FORECAST (99 DADDIES BOOK 3)

CASEY COX

SYNOPSIS

Forecast: (noun)
A calculation or estimate of future events, especially coming weather.
See also: Liam "I'm Always Right" Wright.

Not your typical Daddy. Not your typical boy.
Not your typical fake relationship.

Hudson Madden looks like the kind of guy you don't want to piss off—he's a walking wall of muscle, brightly tatted ink up both arms, and low grunts. But underneath it all, he's a gentle giant. One who can't find what he wants because of the assumptions people make:

He must be an alpha.
He must be a dominant Daddy.
He must be looking for a sweet, passive boy.

The truth is more complicated. Haunted by memories of a former lover, and interested in exploring types of sex that aren't easily defined, Hudson is happy to harbour his innocent crush on the local weatherman.

Until said weatherman crush walks into Hudson's gym and turns his life upside down.

Liam "I'm Always Right" Wright. It might be a cute catchphrase, but when it comes to love, Liam is always wrong.

Liam hasn't got time for love. He's got his sights set on the big time, becoming a prime time meteorologist on a major national TV station. He'll do anything it takes to get the promotion, even if it means entering into a fake relationship to improve his chances.

A quick-fix, no-mess solution.

So why does it feel so right when Hudson looks at him, spends time with him, and gets to know him in a way that no one ever has?

Will Hudson be able to break down his walls and let Liam in? And when forced to choose between his career and love, will Liam be able to make the right choice?

FORECAST

Forecast is a Daddy-lite fake relationship MM romance featuring a gentle giant of a Daddy, and an ambitious weatherman.

Come along for the ride and enjoy some crazy/sexy/cool shenanigans involving tantra, multiple orgasms, a heartfelt list of 18 favorite things, a crew of sassy friends, lots of LOLs, and all the feels on the way to a heartwarming HEA.

Forecast is the third book in the *99 Daddies* series. Each book in the series will contain overlapping characters and storylines, so you may enjoy them more by reading them in order.

99 DADDIES

99 Daddies is a hilarious, entertaining, and heartwarming contemporary/new adult Daddy-lite MM romance series.

Escape to Daylesford, the (fictional) Daddy capital of America. If you love steamy and complex Daddy/boy dynamics, May-December gay romances with a twist, sweet and sassy MM age gap romances—and chasing those guaranteed HEAs—you'll love it here.

So come along and meet the 99 Daddies of Daylesford. Who will be YOUR favorite?

PUBLISHER'S NOTE

CHAPTER ONE

HUDSON

"You know, you really do get a lot of hole pics," Porter said, sauntering in to stand beside me at the front desk of my gym.

"You're not meant to be behind here," I grumbled, pointing to the *Staff Only* sign he had just brushed past without even looking, his eyes glued to the cell phone screen in front of him, his fingers manically swiping left and right.

He looked up briefly at the sign and smiled. He peered over at me and his lips stretched even wider. When he glanced back down at the phone, his smile practically fell off his face.

I clenched my jaw and stepped toward him. Just because we'd known each other for over twenty years and he was one of my closest friends, didn't mean he still didn't annoy the living shit out of me sometimes.

Like right about now.

"You're not meant to be behind the counter, Porter," I repeated in a low, but firm, tone.

"What? Oh, that?" He glanced over at the *Staff Only* sign. "Relax, would you? That rule only applies to staff. You're not staff, you own the place. Ooh, look at that pink beauty!"

He gazed downward again. I looked down briefly only to see a closeup of what I guessed was some guy's asshole. An extremely *close* closeup of some guy's asshole.

Wait, where was my phone?

Suddenly my brain clicked into gear as a torrent of rage began to swirl in my belly.

"Porter," I growled. "Are you on my phone?"

I looked around the piles of papers scattered messily across the counter, flicking them up in search of my phone. "I swear to god if you've installed some app..."

"Hudson Madden." Porter's light green eyes widened in my direction.

We both looked at one another, like two lions who had just spotted each other in the wild for the first time, unsure of what would happen next and who would emerge as the dominant one.

Me. I would be the dominant one because I was in no mood for Porter's bullshit.

"I'm offended that you would even think that I would do something like take your phone. That would be such a betrayal of trust."

I pulled open the top drawer under the computer and found it. My phone was sitting there, just where I had left it. I *hmpfed* loudly enough for him to hear it.

Loudly enough for him to break out into a self-satisfied smirk.

Loudly enough for him to walk over the couple of steps to me, lean his self-satisfied face in until he was just a few inches away from me, and say, "No. See, what I did was take a few pics from your social media, cut off the head because no one really gives a shit about that anyway, and set up a fake account on *Gruff*—on my own phone—to see what kind of response *I*, meaning *you*, would get."

The guy was freaking unbelievable.

"Porter." I blurted it out so forcefully that he jumped back, startled. "Why on earth would you do that?"

"Well," he began, straightening his shoulders to regain some of his lost composure. "It's down to you and me now, Hudson."

"What do you mean?" I quirked an eyebrow while checking the phone in the drawer to make sure it really was mine and not some dummy phone he'd switched it with. Hey, I couldn't afford to let my guard down with this guy.

The screen lit up and the image of a smiling Lisa Kudrow and Mira Sorvino beamed back at me. Relief. I smiled for a brief moment. *Romy and Michele's High School Reunion* really was the best movie of all time.

My smile quickly turned to a scowl when Porter started talking again.

"Well," he said, turning to face me as his expression grew more serious. He was still dressed in his all-black workout gear and his skin was covered in a light mist of post-workout sweat. "Stirling has got Mikey."

"Yes, he does," I said, genuinely happy for the guy. "They're coming up on a year together now."

"Really?" Porter seemed somewhat surprised. "Goes to show you how quickly time flies."

I nodded as he continued, "And Steel has Nick now, so we barely see him anymore either."

There was a slight undertone of something in Porter's voice that I couldn't quite make out. It wasn't jealousy or resentment, maybe it was...longing?

"From what I hear, Steel *deffers* has his hands full with Nick," I said with a knowing grin.

"Oh yeah, for sure," Porter agreed, flopping down into one of the spare chairs behind the counter. "That boy is one helluva brat...in the best possible way, of course."

We both chuckled while I made a mental note to check in with Steel to make sure he was really okay the next time I saw him.

Porter started spinning himself around aimlessly in the chair as I mulled over his words. He had a point. Both of our closest friends were in relationships. We were the last two single Daddies standing.

But was that really such a bad thing?

Porter was happy the way he was. At least, I thought he was. He got plenty of action. Between all the apps he was on and the amount of time he spent at Revolver, Daylesford's most exclusive BDSM club, he had no shortage of explicit sexscapades to fill me in on. He was looking for fun and fucking, nothing more serious.

Kind of like me. Well, except for the fun and fucking part. Come to think of it, I wasn't looking for much of anything at all, really.

"So what has the fact that we're the last two single Daddies left in the quad squad got to do with you creating a fake account for me on *Gruff*?" I said, returning to my original question.

Silence. When Porter spoke, he was so quiet I had to move in just to hear him.

"I just love you and I'm worried about you, Hudson."

Damn him. I *hmpfed* again.

That was the thing about Porter Jones: even when he crossed the line—and boy, had he done that plenty over the two decades we'd been friends—underneath it all, there really was a good guy. One of the best, actually.

"Delete the app," I said, but the bite in my voice was gone.

"I will, I will," Porter said with a sigh as he grabbed the phone and began tapping away.

I'd never been a big fan of apps. I knew plenty of people who had met their person on them, so I knew they worked. It wasn't in any way a judgment. Trust me, I'm the least judgmental guy you'll ever meet.

It was probably just a *me* thing. I needed that face-to-face connection with someone that you only got when you saw them in person, not in a small thumbnail image on a screen.

*You know you're forty when...*right?

Besides, I'd never had a good experience on apps the few times I had tried them. Apps were too restrictive for someone like me. They reduced you to a few limited labels: top, bottom, or switch.

What if you didn't fit into any of those predefined labels? What then?

You got blocked, abused, and deleted, that's what.

Heck, dating wasn't any easier. I'd had a couple of semi-serious relationships, but my last relationship had been the biggest, most serious one.

Richie came into the gym one day on a New Year's health kick, hellbent on turning his life around. His curly ginger hair and easy smile had melted me from the moment he walked through the front door.

He was wickedly cute, smart, thoughtful, complicated, and tortured. Very tortured.

We were good together in so many ways, and then in a few ways, we were totally incompatible. We had our fair share of problems. Issues that we both worked hard to overcome. But ultimately, Richie's demons got the better of him and he ended his life.

He'd come into the gym to not only improve his physical health, but his mental health as well. I felt as if I had failed him. I *had* failed him. The guilt and the burden overwhelmed me. But with the support of my closest friends—Porter, Steel, and Stirling—as well as eighteen months in therapy, I made progress. Baby steps, but still progress.

"Do you still, you know, visit?" Porter's words snapped me back to reality. He had a freakish way of knowing what was on my mind.

"You mean Richie?" I asked. The words felt heavy in my throat. Porter nodded.

"Yeah, just once a month. Bring some new flowers, make sure the gravestone is clean and tidy, that sort of thing, you know?"

"That's so nice that you do that," Porter got up and gave me a hug. I let him lean into my body for a moment.

Again, at times like this, the decency of the guy shone through.

As did his disgusting sweatiness, which I could feel against my skin.

"Get off me, you're all wet. Have you even showered?" I asked, pushing him away with a lighthearted laugh.

"Of course I have," he replied indignantly. He bit down on his lip and moved in again, yet staying far enough away from me not to warrant another push. "I have noticed that I've been sweating a lot more and for a lot longer after each workout since I turned forty. Is that normal, Hudson?"

I let out a deep laugh. "There is nothing normal about you, Porter. And stop distracting me. How are you doing with deleting *Gruff*?"

He sulked back over to grab his phone, his brows pinched tightly together as he gawked at the screen.

"They make it really tough. I can't find a way to delete it in any of the settings." He looked up, saw my face, and quickly looked back down again. "But don't worry, I'll find it."

"Yeah, you better," I said, starting to feel the irritation boiling up inside of me again. "I want that thing deleted before you leave here tonight."

I could have sworn I heard him mutter something about him being the Dom and not me, but I let it slide.

"Hey, boss."

I turned in the direction of the deep male voice. It was shortly followed by a friendly female voice.

"Hey, Hudson."

"Hey, Teddy. Hey, Stephanie," I said, greeting them with a warm smile as they ran their club passes through the machine. "Have a great workout, guys."

"Mmm, mmm, mmm." Porter's lip-smacking assaulted my ears and his still-sweaty palm landed on my shoulder. "Who were *they*?" His tongue hung loosely out the side of his mouth.

"That was Teddy and Stephanie," I said, worming my way from underneath his disgustingly clammy hand and moving a few steps away.

"What I wouldn't give to see his hole," Porter said, his eyes following Teddy as he walked over to the warm-up area as he began doing some inadvertently suggestive stretches, bending over from the waist and revealing his perfectly pert ass.

"I think Stephanie might have something to say about that," I said with a snicker.

"I'm sure she wouldn't mind sharing...or watching. A lot of people are into that these days, you know?" Porter said, tilting his head to the side as Teddy did a ridiculous-looking stretch that even made me tilt my head for a better view.

He was a very fit man, a former football player who still possessed an impressive physique and very, *very* muscular legs that were now, somehow, above his head.

"Besides," Porter said. His lips were moving, but his eyes weren't. They were still firmly transfixed on Teddy. "What straight guy calls another guy *boss*?"

I rolled my eyes even though I knew he wouldn't notice.

"It's like calling a guy *man* or *dude*. Plenty of straight guys say it," I said.

"Yeah, well I wish they'd say it to me."

I managed to snap myself out of the Teddy-trance, happy to leave Porter lingering in his for a moment or two longer. I could only imagine the filthy thoughts running through his mind.

"Alright, back to deleting the app please," I said after a few moments had passed, giving him a tap on his wet shoulder.

He moved over to the phone and sat back down again slowly. He put his feet up on the counter—another pet peeve of mine, but I didn't say anything. If it got him to delete the app, I could live with it.

"Can't blame a guy for looking," he said. I thought he was talking about Teddy until I walked up behind him and saw a smooth, puckered hole filling the screen.

"Hey, you're meant to be deleting the app," I growled. "Besides, technically those photos are for me, not for you."

"You're no fun," he said as I pushed his feet off the counter. They landed on the floor with a heavy thud.

"You know I don't like that," I said, ignoring his scowl.

"Hey, it's not my fault. I never get this many hole pics. Let me enjoy it for a minute," he protested.

"You don't?"

"Nope, never," he replied with a firm head shake.

"So, how come I get so many?" I asked.

He quirked an eyebrow at me.

"Do I really need to spell it out for you?" he asked.

Clearly, he did.

"You've got total alpha vibes happening, Hudson. People take one look at you—your massive muscles, your tattoo sleeves, your shaved head—they see all of that and they've got you pegged."

Ha, if only they knew.

"And they want it," he continued. "That's why all these thirsty bottoms are sending you pics, *like these*," he said as he pointed a photo of a hairy, open hole at me.

"Put that away," I said, looking around, praying there were no customers milling about. This was precisely the reason why the front counter was a *Staff Only* area. Maybe I should just replace the sign with a *No Porter* one instead.

I sulked over to the other side of the counter to create some space between Porter and myself. His irritating words echoed in my head. He was right, though, which irritated me even more. People did look at me and instantly have their minds made up.

I had to be this, or I had to be into that...

They were always wrong. No one had ever figured me out yet. Not even Richie.

I looked out at the gym floor. Apart from Teddy and Stephanie, there were only about half a dozen other people working out. I let out a depressed sigh, rubbing my eyes, hoping that as if by magic, I'd reopen them to find the gym packed full of people like it used to be. Like all three of my gyms used to be until the year from hell happened.

I'd been forced to close down two of my gyms. I was down to just this one, and it wasn't doing so great either.

Maybe it was life's way of telling me to move on? Who knew...

I glanced up at the clock on the wall. Shit, it was almost eight. I flew by a stunned Porter who looked at me like I was an alien as I lunged for the remote controls. I grabbed one in each hand and began flicking each of the eight TV screens that were perched above the cardio area over to channel nine.

He'd be on in a moment.

Eight was the last forecast he'd do that night, before they switched to...whoever did the weather forecasts for the rest of the night. I actually had no idea who that was because I stopped paying attention as soon as he was done.

"What are you doing?" Porter asked.

I was frantically trying to make the remote reach all the TVs, but the two farthest away were always a struggle. I flailed my arms in their direction, pressing down as hard as I could with my fingers until, finally, the channels both changed and there he was.

Liam "I'm Always Right" Wright.

My face softened and I may have let out a soft coo...

Liam was wearing a checkered navy blue and black shirt with the sleeves rolled up—I loved when he rolled his sleeves up, revealing a peek of the light brown hairs smattered across his arms —and a pair of tight-fitting gray dress pants. *Very* tight-fitting pants.

That was kind of his thing, I guess. The look he was known for because, despite looking lean and in shape otherwise, his ass was the size of two balloons.

While I could admit it was a damn fine ass, that wasn't what drew me to him. He just had a niceness about him. He seemed sweet and interesting. He was genuinely passionate about the weather. He cracked terrible weather jokes which only he—and I—laughed at. He had a slightly crooked incisor tooth which was purely adorable.

"You still crushing on the weatherman?" Porter said. I could hear the smile in his voice, even though I didn't turn away from the TV screens. Yes, I still had my crush on him, and frankly, I didn't care what anyone else thought about it. I was actually enjoying the feeling.

I'd seen the guy out and about exactly six times, and I'd frozen and been unable to approach him exactly six times.

Maybe I was a total chickenshit, but I actually think it had more to do with the fact that my crush on him was comfortable *for me*. It was exactly what I needed. Seeing him with the distance a TV screen—or eight—perked me up every day. It made me smile. And it wasn't anything more than a harmless crush. It was perfect for me.

"Fine, the app's deleted," Porter's voice rang out.

"Good," I said firmly. My eyes were still locked on the sexiest weatherman in Daylesford—no wait, scratch that, the entire country.

"Uh...boss?"

This time it wasn't Teddy, but my employee Zander's voice that finally managed to draw my attention away from the TVs.

"What is it?" I snapped, sounding rougher than I had intended.

Zander's eyes widened in surprise and he took half a step back.

"Sorry," I quickly added. "What's up?"

Zander was one of my best workers and a very popular, and highly qualified, personal trainer.

He scratched his neck, avoiding looking at me directly.

"Why are all the TVs on channel nine? A few clients are...well, complaining." He finally looked up and he seemed relieved when he saw my face and could tell I wasn't going to kill him.

"I don't care, I'm watching this," I said, suddenly realizing how douchey that made me sound.

"Eh, boss, business has been a little slow lately. Maybe we shouldn't piss off the clients we do have," Zander said.

I grumbled under my breath.

He was right.

"Tell 'em I'll change it back in five, okay?"

That seemed to satisfy him and he bolted from the reception area and back out onto the gym floor.

"Hmm, I wouldn't mind seeing his hole either," Porter said as his eyes hungrily followed Zander.

"Porter," I said, trying to restrain myself. "You are officially banned from using the word *hole*."

My eyes returned to the TVs...all eight of them.

All filled with him.

"I don't even get why you like him," Porter continued talking, following my eyes to the TVs. "I mean, sure he's got a nice ass and I'm sure his ho—entrance is mighty fine too, but he's in the media, Hudson. That's a red flag for me. He's gotta be a jerk."

I kept my gaze glued to the screens.

"You just don't like the media because you're in politics, so that's not a fair statement," I retorted.

"Besides, from what I hear, he's a total party boy. So totally not your type, Hudson," Porter continued, trying to bait me.

Nothing a little middle finger wouldn't fix.

"Shut up, Porter," I added for good measure.

"And that's the weather forecast you know you can always trust, Daylseford, because I'm Liam "I'm Always Right" Wright, signing off for the evening."

I closed my eyes softly as a gentle heat permeated my entire body.

And then begrudgingly, one by one, I changed the channels back again. I would change them all again when Liam came back on tomorrow, wearing his too-tight pants, making his slightly unfunny weather jokes, and finishing off with that cute catchphrase of his.

CHAPTER TWO

LIAM

"And...we're out," the line producer yelled out as I unpinned my mic from the lapel of my jacket.

God, how I hated that stupid catchphrase.

It followed me everywhere I went. I'd have complete strangers coming up to me and not ask for an autograph or a selfie, but for me to say the damn thing. I was quickly becoming a dancing monkey, or meteorologist, to be more accurate.

The lights around me faded to black just as my publicist, Parker Thompson, strode confidently toward me.

"Great job, Liam."

He would say it in a way that appeared friendly, but it always left me feeling a little unnerved.

"Let's talk in your dressing room. I've got news."

My eyes lit up with excitement as I threw the mic onto an empty desk.

"About the promotion?" I asked, but his back was already turned.

"Dressing room," Parker said over his shoulder.

We quickly made our way off the soundstage, zipped down the hallway into the second-to-last door on the right, and into my dressing room.

"Is it about the promotion?" I asked again as soon as he'd closed the door behind us. "Good news, bad news, what? Tell me, Parker. Tell!"

Wake Up America was the country's highest-rated morning news show. They were actively looking for a new addition to their weather team. Just quietly of course, nothing was official or being made public yet.

But Parker was the best publicist in town for a reason. He'd gotten the inside scoop a few weeks back and we had adjusted our game plan accordingly.

"Sit," Parker said, pointing his head to the well-worn couch in the corner of the dressing room. "I've got a list of things to talk to you about."

I walked over to the couch and sat down, my eyes glued to him. He was an attractive guy in an odd way. Or an odd guy in an attractive way. Hard to tell.

He had sandy-blond hair, a good complexion, and rosy red cheeks, but he wore a pair of odd-shaped, black-rimmed glasses— they were straight along the top, but blew out into uneven circles on the bottom. They were distracting and hid his blue eyes, which were actually friendly and welcoming. He was taller and leaner than I was too.

At twenty-nine, Parker was only two years older than me, but he was just as determined to get out of Daylesford as I was. The city was great and all, I was born here and I loved it, but nothing could change the fact that it was a local market. Yes, the fourth largest in the country, but still local. I wanted, no, I *needed* national exposure, especially if I was going to have any chance of...

"No direct news on the promotion yet," he began, sitting down in the equally well-worn chair across from me.

"Damn it," I said with a huff.

Why was it taking so long? I was Daylesford's leading meteorologist. Officially. I had won the local news award for best meteorologist for the last three years.

I'd even straightened and lightened my hair to an almost-but-not-quite blond, heeding the network's call to be more "boy-next-door approachable." I was easy to work with, a team player, and I knew the studio executives all liked me.

Plus, the weather ratings were at an all-time high, even higher than the two segments preceding it. That meant that people tuned in just for the weather.

Just for me.

But I didn't have a big head about it, because I knew that most of it—no, wait, all of it—was due to Parker. The tight pants that showed off my inexplicably round ass were his idea. Waistcoat Wednesdays and Rate My Shirt Saturdays were also his ideas. Wearing a colorful bow tie every once in a while, yep, his idea too.

Even that goddamn stupid catchphrase, *I'm always right*, was his idea.

"Let's go through the list, shall we?" he said, looking at me as he scrunched his nose.

I could never quite tell if he did it because his glasses were falling down, or he simply shared my disdain for the things we had to do to just get ahead in this crazy business.

If people thought showbiz was tough, meteorology was ten levels crazier. The backstabbing, the cattiness, the constant reminders of the forecasts you got totally wrong. No one ever forgot a thing.

"There's a list?" I asked, settling back into the almond-colored leather sofa. It was probably as old as the station, fraying at the edges.

Parker nodded and proceeded to grab a clipboard and flip a page over.

"Let's start with net positives," he said as his blue eyes scanned the page busily. "We've got your ass."

I silently shuddered. Because, of course that would be the number one thing that people liked about me.

"It's got high approval in all the key demos: the millennials, the gays, and the over seventy-fives." He tapped his fingers along the back of the clipboard and smiled as he looked at me, as if that should be music to my ears.

"Great," I managed to say, while successfully resisting the urge to roll my eyes into the back of my head.

"Word on the street is you're a shoo-in to win *Daylesford's Hottest Derriere*," he said, completely not reading my face at all.

That definitely called for an eye roll. "Calling it a *derriere* doesn't make it any more classy, Parker."

"Who cares about classy?" he retorted instantly. "All we care about is publicity at this point, Liam. We need your face, *and your ass*, plastered everywhere if we're going to have a shot at this promotion."

"I guess..." I said, looking around the dressing room.

I knew the window of opportunity was closing for me. It used to be that older meteorologists were respected for their experience and wisdom. Not the case anymore. Everyone knew that forty meant death. *Wake Up America's* weatherman was thirty-nine...and a half. The poor sap.

"Clothes are good, appearance is good as well," Parker continued, going through his checklist until a small wrinkle formed on his otherwise perfectly smooth forehead. I wondered if he'd had any work done.

"Ah, okay, a few minor issues. Not negative yet, but could turn that way if we don't keep an eye on them."

"What—what are they?" I asked, digging my fingers into the leather seat.

I could feel a heaviness forming in the bottom of my stomach. It was never a nice feeling to know that my appearance would be savaged, even if it was broken down into key demo groups. It didn't make the sting hurt any less.

"Hair," he said. "Could be a little longer. How did everything go at Monday's meeting?"

I sighed. "Fine. Three inches."

Yep, every Monday morning, all the male on-air talent had a hair production meeting where we got our hair measured. Viewers had gotten picky over recent years, and wanted their male anchors, sports presenters, and weathermen to have a certain look...and hair length.

Five inches was the gold standard, usually only attained by the biggest names in the business. Four inches was pretty decent and on par for local news anchors. I had been aiming for three and a half inches, since three was clearly not on.

Parker got up and walked over to me, inspected my head like he was looking at a body in a mausoleum and then sat back down again.

"Let's aim for three and a half, shall we?" he said, scribbling something down on the paper.

"We shall," I sighed.

"The tooth thing we can talk about some other time, it's not a big deal," he said, trying to gloss over it.

"Wait, what tooth thing?" I asked, gripping the couch again, even harder than before.

"Your third tooth to the right is a little crooked," he said as I ran my tongue over it. "Not a big deal, but we'll fix it before we get to *Wake Up America*. Heck, they'll probably even pay for it themselves."

I grimaced. I kind of liked my crooked tooth.

"Anyway, moving on...the catchphrase," he said, taking off his glasses as he pinched the top of his nose. "This one's a head-scratcher. On the one hand, your catchphrase is super meme-able."

I didn't quite catch what he said, I had still been sulking over my crooked tooth.

"Sorry, what? Did you say memorable?" I asked.

"Memorable?" Parker scoffed. "Who even has a memory these days, Liam? No, I said *meme-able,* because if you make something meme-worthy, it will last forever. By which I mean, at least one, maybe two news cycles tops."

"So what's the issue with the catchphrase?" I asked. Last he'd told me, it was super popular in all the key demos.

"This."

He pulled out a piece of paper and handed it to me. It was a bunch of screenshots of me presenting the weather, with slight variations of the catchphrase written across the bottom. So instead of *I'm always right,* I was looking at:

His ass is so tight

Ride him all night

I'd love to take a bite

"We made it too easy," Parker lamented. "We should have gone for something that had fewer rhyming options."

"But then it wouldn't have been as catchy...or as meme-able," I added dryly.

"I know, you're right," Parker said, putting his glasses back on. "We'll just have to monitor it to see how it progresses."

I shook my head and let out a laugh, having to remind myself that this was my actual life. Talking about hair length and memes about my ass.

Never anything real, or serious, or that I actually gave a shit about.

"You know," I began. "There is a climate change protest planned for next weekend."

Parker looked at me and scrunched his nose up again. "So?"

"I'd like to go. You know how much I care about environmental issues, and I think it would be really good for me to try to highlight—"

Parker closed his eyes, let out an obscenely loud snore, and then acted as if he had woken himself up.

"Oh my god, Liam, that was so boring you literally put me to sleep in a nanosecond."

"Parker, I just want to use my platform—"

"Stop," Parker said, lifting his long, thin fingers into the air. "I know what you're going to say. I've heard it a million times before. Environment. Planet. Trees. Climate. I know, it's all important stuff, Liam. I'm, like, all in on it."

I looked at him and strangely, I actually did believe him. I trusted the guy because I knew he genuinely wanted to help me and see me succeed. He was just able to be more serious about the silly things we had to do to get there.

"But, you'll have a much bigger platform once you go national." He stated it like the obvious fact that it was.

"You're right," I said.

"I'm always right," he said in a high-pitched campy tone and we both giggled. "Just hang in there. You're doing everything you're meant to be doing, we just have to wait for the signal. And it's coming, Liam."

"You think so?" I asked, suddenly needing his reassurance more than ever.

"I do," he said. His voice was friendly and had just the right amount of firmness.

He glanced down at his clipboard.

"One last thing," he added. "Mrs. Langley."

I swallowed hard, almost choking on my own breath. Whatever it was, this would be difficult—no, impossible—to get out of.

At ninety-nine years young, Mrs. Langley wasn't just Daylesford's oldest and most-loved resident, she was also a very vocal supporter of the station. She had an opinion about everything, which she wasn't afraid to share in the slightest.

When the set had changed from its signature three tones of blue to a more modern orange and brown palette, she wrote to the editor of *The Daylesford Times*...and the set was changed back the next week.

When the producers brought in standing desks for the anchors to use as part of an internal wellness initiative, she started an online petition to have them seated because people didn't need to stand to deliver the news. She got over ten thousand signatures.

Did I mention she was very vocal?

And when an up-and-coming weatherman, fresh out of college, had started at the station five years ago...she'd taken a massive shine to him.

That weatherman was me. Ever since I started, she had been my biggest, and most vocal, fan.

She had an opinion about everything I did, said, and wore.

Ever since I started Rate My Shirt Saturday, she was always the first person to leave a comment on Facebook.

When I wore a white bow tie after Labor Day, she called in to let me know exactly why that was a mistake.

And when I mispronounced *Kuala Lumpur* live on air during a bit about the monsoons that were affecting the region in a global weather segment, she sent me a card and flowers the next day to cheer me up.

Did I mention she was vocal?

"What is it this time?"

Parker said nothing. He just carefully placed the clipboard on his laptop and raised his right hand into the air beside his face, giving it a Beyonce-style twirl.

"She wants me to do a cover of *Single Ladies?*" I joked.

"You wish," Parker replied. "That would probably be easier and more fun for you than what I'm about to say."

The heavy pit in my stomach rose up into my chest.

"She wants you to put a ring on it...or at least be seeing someone."

"Really?" I said. I hadn't been expecting that.

"She's worried about you, Liam," Parker said seriously, as if he were actually entertaining her feedback. The completely ludicrous feedback.

"I don't have time for a boyfriend, Parker, you know that," I said.

Surely, he of all people would understand that. He spent most of his days trying to figure out how to improve my career. I spent most of my time putting whatever he said I should do into motion. I had little to no time for anything else, much less a boyfriend.

I was perfectly fine with that. My goal—my only goal—was scoring that promotion to national. The promotion would give me an even bigger platform, and with that platform, I could actually make a difference. That was what it all boiled down to. That was why we both did what we did. At least, that was why *I* did what I did. Parker knew that. He knew I had no time to focus on anything else, much less something as trivial as a relationship.

How could he possibly refute that?

"It's Mrs. Langley, Liam," he said with a smirk that showed me he was enjoying this way more than he should have been. "You're not going to be the one to say no to Mrs. Langley, are you?"

He batted his eyelashes at me a few times, just to ram the point in nice and good. He knew as well as I did that I had no choice in the matter.

I must have looked like a deer in headlights because Parker took pity on me by saying, "You don't have to find someone straight away, Liam. Mrs. Langley's no fool. She knows that love takes time, but just think about it, okay? It doesn't even have to be real, maybe ask a friend or someone you know to be your fake boyfriend for a while. It will make her happy, but it will also look really good for your promotion."

"It will?" I asked, chewing on my bottom lip.

Parker nodded. "Hell yeah, man. The only thing hotter than a hot weatherman, is a hot weatherman with a hot husband...at least, that's what twenty-four to thirty-eights are telling us in the testing."

Of course, it always came down to the testing.

"Anyways, I have to go," Parker said, standing up.

"Hot date?" I asked with a chummy grin. Parker had even less of a social life than I did.

"I've actually started seeing a new guy," Parker said with a smile. "He's got an unusual name. Netflix. But let's just say, I know how to turn him on."

I groaned. "At least I leave my terrible jokes on-air."

As he walked past me, he tousled his hand in my three-inch hair and said, "Don't go on social media. It's a horrible, nasty wormhole. I haven't had a chance to delete all the dick pics on your accounts. I'll do it tomorrow. See you then."

"See you, Parker."

And with that he was gone.

I fished out my cell phone before the door had even closed behind him. I knew I shouldn't do it. It was a terrible habit I had gotten into, but it was also strangely addictive.

Reading random people's comments about you.

Or, as was the case ever since I had started wearing the ridiculously tight pants about a year ago, scrolling through a sea of never-ending dick pics.

It wasn't the pics that did anything for me. A dick was a dick. Once you'd seen about five hundred of them, they all started to look the same.

No, the reason I trawled through the comments section was for the odd and very occasional *diamond in the rough* comment.

A kid who looked up to me and decided to study science or math because *I* liked science and math.

Or a teenager in a small town who felt different and in some way, saw part of themselves when they looked at me, an out-and-proud gay man.

Or someone who used to doubt facts about the real state of the environment, and based on something I'd said, had looked into it and changed their mind.

That's why I did it. That's why I subjected myself to the insane scrutiny of my ass, hair, and teeth, why I wore ridiculously tight pants and super colorful bow ties, and why I uttered that corny catchphrase at the end of each forecast.

To be able to touch someone's life, someone that I'd never even meet in person, was truly a magical thing. And if I could touch their lives and get them to make just one small positive change, it would make the world a better place.

That was all I really wanted. To make a small, positive difference in the world.

I sank back into the sofa and considered it...a fake boyfriend. Maybe I should do it? If it helped me snag that promotion, and made Mrs. Langley happy, what's the worst thing that could happen?

CHAPTER THREE

HUDSON

"I've locked everything up and switched the alarm system to night mode."

I looked up and saw Zander's muscular frame taking up the entire doorway to my office.

"That's great, thank you," I said. "Come on in for a sec."

I quickly saved the document I was working on. It was a dizzying blur of digits and an even more dizzying sea of red.

Zander sat down in the chair across from me. "What's up, boss?"

For a brief moment, I was reminded of my conversation with Porter earlier that evening, but the fact that Zander was gay meant that he was just using the term because it described who I was to him. His boss. His boss who had acted badly toward him before.

I looked at him. He was in his early thirties, and he had a friendly face and a sculpted, muscular body. No tattoos though, despite my gentle insistence that they would look great on him. He was wearing the same all-black uniform I was.

"I'd like to apologize about earlier," I said.

A frown crossed Zander's forehead. "Earlier?"

"Yeah, about the whole TV thing. I was rude to you and I could tell that I made you feel uncomfortable. You were just doing your job, telling me what clients were telling you, probably because they were too afraid to tell me themselves."

His pensive smile confirmed that I was on the right track.

"You've got a lot going on, boss," he said.

"I do," I said with a nod. "But that's still no excuse. You're one of my best employees and I am sorry for the way I spoke to you before."

"Well, thanks for saying so. That's very nice of you," Zander said. He opened and closed his mouth a few times, struggling to find the words he wanted to say.

"Just ask. You remind me of the goldfish I had growing up when you do that thing with your mouth," I said, and we both laughed.

The last traces of laughter vanished from his face as he chewed on his lip and asked, "How bad is it here? I mean, I know you've had to shut down the other two locations, and business has been slow here too, so I'm just worried that..."

His voice trailed off.

"It's not good," I said bluntly. "I'm not going to lie to you, but please keep this to yourself."

Zander nodded. I knew I could trust him. He'd been with me for over five years and had proven his loyalty, as well as his discretion, numerous times.

"Like so many other businesses, we've been hit hard and we're bleeding pretty badly. I've consolidated as much as I can, and reduced all reducible costs, but there are outgoings that we still have to pay. And we're not even breaking even at this point."

"Wow." Zander nodded his head slowly, taking in everything I was telling him. "I knew things were bad, I just didn't realize they were this bad."

His words hit me heavily and I felt the searing shame of failure creep down my chest and settle in my gut. I really had done everything I possibly could have to save my business.

Closing down two locations was heartbreaking for me. It meant letting go of staff, people that I genuinely cared about and who would now be struggling to find other work. It meant saying goodbye to the small band of remaining loyal clients who couldn't travel from the suburbs of Daylesford to the downtown gym. I'd known some of them for years, decades in a few cases, since my days on the weightlifting squad at Daylesford University.

The downtown gym was by far the most popular of the three locations, and it was our best shot at surviving. As heart-wrenching as it was, I knew I'd made the right decision from a business standpoint.

From a human standpoint, well, that was another matter.

After a moment, Zander began to speak, outlining all of the different ways we could possibly try to turn things around.

"We could do an open day..." he began. His words faded into the background.

I couldn't help but blame myself for the business going downhill. Over the past two years, my heart just hadn't been in it anymore.

After Richie died, it was my saving grace. My sanctuary. The place I would come to and be surrounded by people I knew. Those first two years were the hardest of my life. His death, and the way he died, sent me to a very dark place. One that was incredibly hard to climb back out of.

The hardest part, in amongst all the grief and anguish, was pondering the unanswered questions. There were so many things that I wanted to find out, and knowing that I'd never be able to find out was devastating.

He left me a letter. In it, he wrote a line that stayed with me to this very day.

This isn't because of you...

I tried to convince myself that he meant it in the good way, in the kind of way that would make me not blame myself for his actions. But part of me couldn't help but be crushed by those words.

On the surface it'd seemed that we had the most wonderful relationship. Funnily, both Stirling and I were dating guys called Richard at the same time. So Porter came up with the ingenious distinction of calling Stirling's Richard *bad Richard*—because the guy was a lying, cheating scumbag, so, fair enough—and my Richard *good Richard*.

It would piss Stirling off no end and it made me uncomfortable too.

My relationship had looked good on the surface. It was always so important to Richie that other people thought that we were in a good place, even though underneath it all, we fought like crazy, were incompatible in some pretty major ways, and had many unresolved issues. And then, two weeks before he did what he did, we broke up.

Or rather, I ended it.

That was the right decision. I knew it in my heart of hearts, but it only made what he did next even harder to bear. Richie begged me not to tell our friends, family, or anyone else about the breakup. I figured it was the least I could do to give him some time to get used to it, so I agreed. But it meant that when he died, people still thought that we were together.

A shitstorm on top of a shitstorm on top of a shitstorm.

But the gym, therapy, my three closest friends, and my family got me through the next two years. When I finally came out of the grieving process, I looked at my life, and the things that mattered to me, very differently. I knew then that my heart wasn't in the gym anymore.

Yes, I still wanted to help people, but I wasn't interested in just physical health anymore. Mental health became a lot more interesting to me. I wanted to do something good in that space.

What, where, how, and when...I was still in the process of figuring all of that stuff out.

First things first, I had a gym to save.

"So, whaddya think?" Zander asked, his lips curled upward in a hopeful smile.

"Uh, yeah, sure," I said, without the faintest idea of what I was *yeah sure-ing* to.

"Well, which one of my ideas to help promote the gym do you think we should start with, then?"

Damn, I really should have been paying more attention. Luckily, I was saved by the nighttime doorbell ringing. I looked at the time; it was quarter past eleven. Kinda late for a walk-in, but it got me out of the conversation, so I leaped to my feet.

"Tell you what," I said to Zander, who also got up. "Start with one idea, your choice, whatever you think will work best, and let's go from there, yeah?"

"Thanks, boss," he said. "I really think it's influencer marketing. That's so big right now. Everyone is on social media, and I think if we get a good name, someone to really represent the brand well, it could be a huge thing for us."

"Yeah, yeah, that sounds great."

I opened the door to my office, which was only a few feet behind the front desk. I pushed the button to let the latecomer in and stood at the desk, ready to greet them. I looked over my shoulder to see Zander following me.

"It's late," I said to him. "I'm happy to handle this if you want to go..."

"Hello?"

My ears pricked up at the familiarity of that voice.

I snapped my head around and there he was, not on all eight TV screens as I was used to seeing him, but just one person standing right in front of me, on the other side of my front desk.

Liam "Am I Seeing This Right?" Wright.

"Oh, hey, look, Hudson, it's that guy you always make us turn every TV screen over to wa—"

My elbow found Zander's side, and thankfully, that just so happened to be where his *shut the fuck up* button was located.

"Hello," I said in as normal a voice as I could muster.

What the hell was happening here? How was it that Liam Wright was standing right in front of me, looking all sorts of weatherman-gorgeous? He must have come directly from the studio, because he was wearing the same outfit he'd had on earlier in the evening.

Suddenly, I wished that the counter wasn't so high so that I could look down and get a better view of his amazing...

I snapped myself out of that inappropriate, unprofessional thought by saying, "How—how can I help you?"

I tried to smile. I think I might have been smiling. I couldn't tell. I couldn't feel my face, or my feet, or my hands, anymore.

This was precisely the reason why I had avoided approaching him six times before. I was turning to mush.

"I'd like to join the gym," he said. His voice just sounded so familiar, which I guess made sense, since I'd been hearing it every day on the news for the last eighteen months. "Oh, and I'll need a personal trainer as well."

Was it possible to be both floored and speechless at the same time? The answer to that question was a resounding *hell yes*. Trust me, it was coming from a guy who was on the floor, unable to speak.

"We can definitely arrange that," I said after a much-too-long silence. My eyes were glued to him as my hand tapped around the counter, desperately searching for the paperwork and a pen.

"Here you go," I said, once I had finally found them. I looked down and was surprised to see my hands trembling. I quickly pulled them back and placed them firmly on the counter.

Why the hell was I shaking?

I mean, I had seen the guy in the flesh six times before. Although now that I thought about it, every time I had seen him, I'd started to shake and feel a little light-headed. I'd just assumed that was because Porter was around, and he tended to have a mildly nauseating effect on people.

"Do you have a trainer available? I'd like to start as soon as possible. Preferably tomorrow morning, please," Liam said as he looked up from the paperwork he was filling out.

"Yes, of course," I said, and then my brain left my head because the next words out of my mouth were, "My name is Hudson Madden. I'm the owner of Elite Fitness, and I would love to turn you on..."

Shitty shit, shit, shit!

I cleared my throat. "*Take* you on."

Liam's gaze remained focused on the paperwork, so hopefully, he hadn't heard my slip-up. Zander, on the other hand, had clearly heard it, judging by the wicked gleam in his eye.

"Are you sure, boss?" he asked with a smile, putting his hand on my shoulder.

"Of course I'm sure," I said, delicately and discreetly taking his hand off my shoulder and shoving it sharpy behind his back.

His smile widened. "It's just that, you know, you haven't taken on a new client in years."

Liam's head snapped up and his eyes darted between the two of us.

"Is there a problem?" he asked.

Yeah, I was about to fire my best employee if he didn't shut the fuck up.

"No problem at all," I said, taking the paperwork from Liam. Our fingers didn't even touch, and damn if that didn't disappoint me way more than it should have. I barely glanced at the paperwork. "This all looks good, what time would you like to start tomorrow?"

"I work midday to eight, so I need to be in the studio by ten. How does eight sound?" He made every word sound like perfection.

"Eight is great," I said, with a little too much breathiness for my liking.

"Are you okay?" Liam asked. His dark gray eyes bore into my soul.

"Never better, why?" I gulped. And smiled. And tried to stand up a little taller.

"No reason," he said. "You just look a little...pale?"

"I'm all good," I said, silently willing the color back to my face.

"Alright, so I guess I'll see you tomorrow then?" Liam said cheerfully.

"You will indeedly."

Oh god, I had just used the word *indeedly*.

Was that even a word?

And this time, I could tell that he'd heard.

Color was returning to my face—a deep beetroot red.

I kept the closest thing to a smile that I could on my lips as Liam turned around and walked out. I was so embarrassed that I almost forgot to check out his amazing ass as he left. Almost. Hey, I am human after all, and that ass was out-of-this-world spectacular.

"Oh my God," Zander exclaimed once Liam had left. "This is freaking unbelievable. We were just talking about this!"

"Talking about what?"

Even though he'd left, my eyes were still fixated on the now closed front doors Liam had walked through only moments ago.

"Influencer marketing. This will be so good for the gym, Hudson. If we can get Liam Wright to tag us in a few posts, man, that will bring people in like crazy."

Influencer...tag...huh?

My mind was like Liam, it had left the building.

How did I even begin to process standing face-to-face and talking with Liam Wright?

"Oh, and boss," Zander said, the teasing tone in his voice waking me up. "I'm no expert at this sort of thing, but have you got a thing for Liam Wright?"

I turned to him and tried to summon my most stern face. "No, I do not have a *thing* for Liam Wright. I just happen to enjoy the weather and I think he does a great job of...bringing it to life."

"Yeah, I can see you do," Zander said, with laughter erupting from his mouth as he pointed at my groin.

My hard-on was pushing my shorts out so far I was surprised I hadn't burst through the flimsy material.

"It's all good, boss," he said as he walked past me. "I happen to like the sports presenter, Dan Adams, the way you like the weatherman, so I know what you're going through."

He had no idea what I was going through...because I had no freaking idea myself.

How did I go from admiring Liam Wright from the safe distance of eight TV screens, to having a personal training session with him the very next day?

I swallowed hard. I looked down at my hands and my fingers had started trembling again.

What had I just gotten myself into?

CHAPTER FOUR

LIAM

"Alright, three more," Hudson's deep, gentle voice filled my ears. I was flat on my back and the man was towering over me like the Leaning Tower of Pisa.

Three more?

This whole *lifting weights up and down* thing was way harder than it looked.

I let out a small groan and lifted the heavy bar from the middle of my chest, up away from me as steadily as I could. My arms were already starting to shake. How freaking embarrassing. The guy must have thought I was a complete weakling. I *was* a complete weakling.

Despite having an inexplicably huge ass that would make any Kardashian proud, I had never set foot in a gym in my entire adult life. Until now.

Hudson placed his hands in the middle of the bar as I lowered it. That helped with the shaking. My heart was already racing, I was sweating profusely, and on top of all of that, I was tired as hell.

I had barely gotten a wink of sleep last night. I had been tossing and turning constantly, my thoughts racing about the promotion and what Parker and I could do to make sure that I got it. It had nothing at all to do with the six-foot-six, three-hundred-pound tower of muscle that was currently leaning over me.

No, nothing at all.

His sexy shaved head. His bright, intricate tattoos covering every square inch of both arms. Green eyes that looked like a field in the Swiss Alps. Okay, so maybe even if I did think a little bit about him, ever since I had stepped into the gym this morning, he had been the epitome of pure professionalism.

"One more. Come on, this is the last one. You can do it," he said, and for some reason, hearing his words helped me find an extra reserve of untapped strength to lift that stupid bar up and down one more time.

He grabbed the weight off me once I was done and effortlessly put it back onto the two hookie things it rested on. Like it was no big deal. I guess for a guy his size, lifting a hundred pounds wasn't a big deal. He could probably do it in his sleep. My arms, on the other hand, were already sore—in addition to shaky—and we had only just started.

"Here," Hudson said, handing me my water bottle. "Take a few smaller sips. We'll do another round in sixty seconds."

His voice was so strong and commanding, it sent a gentle tingle across my skin.

"I thought you said that was the last one," I said in between taking small sips of water as he'd instructed.

"It was the last one," he said, as he broke out into a smile. "Of that set."

What the hell's a set?

I nodded anyway. The man probably already thought I was a

weakling, I didn't need him to think that I was a *completely clueless* weakling at that.

I looked him up and down, as discreetly as I could. Just like last night, he was dressed in all black. It must have been the gym uniform. Black shoes, black socks, black shorts, and a very tight-fitting black polo that had the words *Elite Fitness* just above the square pocket on the front of the shirt.

I couldn't help but stare at his beautiful tattoos. I normally wasn't into guys with tattoos. Heck, with my crazy schedule, I wasn't into guys at all.

Yep, at twenty-seven, I was still technically a virgin. Unless jacking off with a friend in high school and getting blown by a former roommate counted. But as for sex, as in real sex, yeah, I was a total loser—I mean, virgin.

I huffed into my water bottle and glanced over at Hudson's arms again.

But Hudson's tattoos. Something about them drew me in, and it wasn't just the vivid, bold colors or the intricacy of the work. I felt like there was a story behind them. A story I was keen to hear.

What was the etiquette for talking to a personal trainer in between *sets*? Was it allowed, frowned upon, or what? I didn't know, and I was getting a whole bunch of mixed signals from the guy.

When I'd walked in last night, he'd seemed kind of nervous and unsure of himself. I figured he was just tired after a long day. But then that Freudian slip. That was the mother of all Freudian slips. Was it a slip, or just a sign of a tired mind?

But then this morning, he was all professional. Sure, friendly and smiley, but no Freudian slips. At least not yet, although a part of me was strangely hoping for one.

Before I could even begin to think about it, his voice boomed down on me. "Alright, let's go again. Ten more. Come on Liam, you can do this."

My name sounded good on his lips.

Somehow, this set went by faster and felt a little easier.

"Good job," Hudson said again, handing me the water bottle.

This time, though, our fingers grazed as he gave it to me, and it sent a warm fluttery sensation into my stomach. I looked up at him briefly and it looked like he had flinched, ever so slightly.

"Another rest and then we'll do one more set," he said, his voice cracking on the last word. He cleared his throat and smiled at me as I sipped on the water.

"So, uh, how did you get into...sorry, I don't know the proper name for it. Weathering?" he asked, scratching behind his neck as a slight blush overtook his cheeks.

"Meteorology," I said, letting out a laugh.

"Yeah, that," he said. The poor man. The smallest thing could set him off into the biggest blush.

I swirled the remaining water in my mouth, thinking about how to answer his question. Although, really, what was there to think about? I would just give him the same sanitized and well-rehearsed version I had said a million times before. But for just the briefest of moments, I considered telling him the real story, and just as quickly, decided against it.

"I was always an outdoorsy child," I began, trying to inject some freshness into the well-worn speech. "I loved playing outdoors, hiking in the mountains, and swimming at the beach. I guess because of that, I was always acutely aware of the weather, even as a young kid."

I looked over at Hudson. In addition to being a gym owner, the guy should have considered a career in acting, because he looked like he was genuinely fascinated by everything I was saying.

So I continued.

"I became intrigued with how it all worked. Clouds, rain, wind...I began studying it in my own time and I just had a real knack for it, you know?" I normally just kept going with the story, but when I looked over at Hudson and saw him nodding his head furiously, I couldn't help but smile.

"My dad used to golf with Walter Devine. Have you heard of him?" I asked.

Hudson flicked his tongue out as he considered it for a minute. "The name does ring a bell, but I can't place it. Sorry."

"That's okay," I said with a giggle. "He was the senior meteorologist on channel nine, and kind of like, my biggest hero. He got me an internship at the station and I absolutely adored everything about it. I studied meteorology when I finished high school, and then got a very lucky break and was able to follow in my hero's footsteps. It was the best thing I ever did."

End of speech.

Close with a fake smile.

My story was met with an unexpected look from Hudson. Normally, people looked happy at my heartwarming recollection. But for some reason, not Hudson.

Before I could ask why, he said, "Last set, let's go," and I was back down on the bench lifting a hundred pounds, which all of a sudden, felt like the heaviest hundred pounds in the universe.

When I finished the ten torturous movements, I grabbed the water bottle myself and gulped it down until it was almost empty.

Hudson stared at me like he wasn't quite sure what to make of me. His light green eyes darted around my face and I suddenly felt like I was under the glaring heat of the studio lights.

"What is it?" I finally asked. It came out a little snappier than I had wanted, and for a second, Hudson looked taken aback. He quickly recovered and then he sat down on the bench next to me.

"When you talked before, about how you started in *meteorology*..." I smiled at his correction. "I couldn't help but notice that you spoke about it in the past tense. You *adored* it. It *was* the best thing you ever did. Do you not feel that way anymore?"

Holy shit. Who was this man?

It was my turn to be taken aback. My mouth felt dry again and I had no idea how to respond. I wasn't used to people listening to me so intently.

I stood up and did the only thing I could possibly do.

"So, what's the next exercise, then?" I said, although it sounded more like a croak.

Hudson narrowed his eyes at me for a moment, but then he stood up as well. I was just under six feet, and yet the man positively towered over me. And for some reason, I really liked that.

"Squats?" he said, although it came out as more of a question, like the man's brain was still stuck on what he had asked me. The question I had ignored.

"No," I said forcefully. "No squats."

My ass was already big enough as it was. I didn't want to do anything that made it even larger. No, the whole point of me joining the gym was to make the rest of my body catch up to my ass, so that I looked more proportional and then maybe, just maybe, I'd be less known for my ass and more for the thing that I actually did: tell the weather.

"Why not?" Hudson seemed puzzled by my strong reaction.

"Look, Hudson," I said, and I swear I could have heard him take in a sharp inhale as I moved in closer to him. "I came to the gym for one reason and one reason only. I want to...proportionize."

He definitely hadn't been expecting me to say that if the smile on his face was anything to go by.

"Proportionize?" he asked, raising an eyebrow.

Damn it. I was hoping that would be a gym term, like *barbell* or *sets*.

I cleared my throat. I had to ask the man a question, but before I asked, I needed to pre-qualify the question I wanted to ask with two other questions.

"Are you gay?" I asked.

"Yes," he said without the slightest hesitation.

Good. One down, two to go.

"Are you single?" I asked.

This time, he paused and hesitated.

Shit, maybe I'd just broken a golden tenet of the trainer/client relationship. My breath hitched in my throat as I waited for his answer.

"Yes," he finally said. His voice was firm, neutral.

Good. That was the clearance I needed to ask the question I had wanted to ask him.

"Have you seen my ass?" I said, turning around and to my side, basically waving my ass into his line of sight so that if he'd somehow been living under a rock for the past few years and missed it, he would definitely see it now.

To my surprise—and horror—Hudson grimaced and looked away.

What was happening here?

He was a single gay man and the sight of my ass made him squirm like he'd just been asked to eat raw chicken. He was a key demo group, too. It made no sense. Oh god, and now I sounded like Parker...

I turned back around to face him straight on. He lifted his gaze to meet mine.

"I have seen your ass, yes," he said quietly.

At least that was something. I placed a hand on my hip.

"Well, good," I said indignantly. "You know, I'm known for this ass. And there's a rumor that I'm a shoo-in for *Daylesford's Hottest Derriere. A shoo-in.*"

"That's great," he said with literally zero conviction.

"Do you have a problem with my ass?" I asked, stepping toward him.

Hey, I might not have liked all the attention my ass got me, but as I was discovering, I also didn't like it when my ass *didn't* get any attention.

Especially from this man.

"I don't, it's just..." His cheeks were positively on fire by this point.

"Just what?" I said with another step closer to him.

I could smell the whiff of his citrusy deodorant. Or was he more of a body spray guy? I shook my head, it didn't matter right now.

"It's just, well, I mean..." Just when I thought the man was incapable of producing an intelligible sentence, he looked up at me and spoke.

"It's just that your ass is like, I don't know, my eighteenth favorite thing about you. I think there's more to you than just...your ass."

No, seriously, who was this man?

Just as I looked up at him, I saw Hudson and the other trainer I had seen last night looking at each other. The guy was clearly egging him on with his eyes, because when he saw me looking at them, he instantly looked away.

Hudson turned to me and cleared his throat.

"Hey, does tagging mean anything to you?"

"You mean like on social media?" I asked, and Hudson nodded uncomfortably.

"Uh, yeah, do you think you could maybe..."

"Tag the gym and help get you some more publicity?" I said flatly.

Right, so that's what he wanted, why he was acting as if he were kinda sorta maybe interested in me. For publicity.

"I'm sorry, Liam. I shouldn't have asked. It wasn't even my idea, but Zander thought it would help with..."

"Hudson, it's okay," I said as I grabbed his forearm. Both of us looked down at my fingers on his heavily inked forearm.

Then we looked up and our eyes met. A fire tore through me and the only way I could put it out was to stop touching the man. So why didn't I want to do that?

Finally, I did. I grabbed my cell phone for a selfie.

"You ready?" I asked. I wasn't sure if I was asking him or myself.

"Yep," he sounded like he was gulping down a bottle full of water.

I snapped a few selfies and then looked at them. Sure, I could tag the gym. It was no big deal for me, and if it helped Hudson attract more customers, I was more than happy to do the guy a small favor.

As I scrolled through the pictures, I was struck by how photogenic he was. Like, *really* photogenic.

And despite our completely different appearances, we looked good together. Like, *really* good together.

"Oh, Hudson," I said as I looked up at him and put on my best smile. If I was doing the man a favor, surely he could do a small favor for me in return...or for Mrs. Langley, to be more precise? "Would you like to be my fake date for a thing I'm going to next week? It's just one night. We'll only have to pose for a few photos. There's a free open bar. Whaddya say?"

Hudson's face drained of color, and for a moment I was worried the giant man would topple over. Somehow, he regained his composure, cleared his throat, and looked me straight in the eye. After what felt like forever, he finally opened his mouth.

"Yes, I'd love to be your fake date, Liam."

CHAPTER FIVE

HUDSON

I stopped myself before I opened the wood-panelled front door to Porter's house.

Since Steel and Stirling now had their boys, we had come up with a new monthly tradition. Every last Thursday of the month was family night, the original quad squad, plus the two boys. We all took turns hosting, and this month it was at Porter's house.

I turned and leaned against the heavy door frame. I'd have to tell them about Liam. There was no way I could avoid it. But what exactly was I going to say?

In the three days since his personal training session, his presence had drifted in and out of my consciousness like waves gently lapping at the shore. He was always there, sometimes more present, sometimes just in the background. But always there nevertheless.

In some ways, I still didn't feel like I had a good read on the guy. He was as nice, charming, funny, and cute as I had imagined he would be. Okay, maybe the cuteness was in overdrive; not even my wildest imagination could have come up with that.

Which was all well and good, but it was only surface-level stuff. There was something deeper to him as well, I could tell. Although his first time at a gym in his adult life probably wasn't the best time to be asking him deep questions, judging by the way he'd avoided answering them.

I couldn't help it. I was a deeper-level kind of person. Whereas someone like Stirling was quiet because that was just who he was, a quiet guy, I was quiet because I didn't really do that great with chitchat and small talk. It bored me because it was all so inconsequential and ultimately, dull. Real talk fascinated me, but it was hard to go deeper with Liam.

I had been holding back with him too, so that could have had something to do with it. I barely got a wink of sleep the night before our training session. My entire body had been flooded with adrenaline, knowing that I would be training one-on-one with Liam Wright.

I had to bite my tongue—as in I would literally bite down on it —at least two dozen times during his workout, to stop myself from fangirling like some crazed fan.

I sighed as I looked out at Porter's impressive front yard and driveway. I was stalling, but not getting any clearer in my head about what I would tell the guys. Screw it, I'd just wing it and see what happened. Maybe with Nick and Mikey there, the guys would be a little more restrained.

And by *the guys*, I meant *Porter*.

I opened the front door, let myself in, and headed to the sunken living room where I assumed they would all be sitting. I was right. I could hear Porter's voice ringing out. He was excited, and it sounded like he was wrapping up a very long-winded and explicit sex story. I inched toward the edge of the room. Judging by the looks on the guy's faces, I was right.

"So you see, with my ankle on guy number two's shoulder, and with guys one and three standing beside each other, *that's* how I managed to get three dicks in my ass at the same time. My first ever triple penetration."

The pride in Porter's voice was offset by the stunned silence in the room. It was like all the air had been sucked out of it.

Great time to make my entrance.

"Hey guys," I said.

"Hudson," Mikey leaped off the couch he was sharing with Stirling and ran over to me, although I figured he was actually running from Porter's story. I gave everyone a quick round of bear hugs—Stirling, Steel, Nick, and finally Porter.

"Did I miss anything?" I asked with a low laugh. "That sounded like quite the story."

I made my way over to sit beside Steel and Nick on the couch.

"I was just talking to the guys about geometry," Porter said.

My eyes narrowed in suspicion.

"That didn't sound very geometrical to me," I said.

Porter huffed and raised his glass.

"He really does look like Samantha from *Sex and the City* sometimes, doesn't he?" Nick said, gently rubbing his elbow against me.

"Looks, talks, and acts like a Samantha. A total Samantha," Steel said as we all broke out into laughter.

"Well I don't mind," Porter said, giving a very Samantha shimmy and shrug. "I'm not going to apologize for finding a sexual application for geometry."

More laughter followed, with Porter joining in. He always pretended not to like our ribbing and *Sex and the City* references, but the truth was...he was a terrible actor. He always ended up laughing at himself and the silliness of it all.

He was as much in on the joke as the rest of us were.

"So how's everyone else doing?" I asked, looking around at my friends. "Geometrical discoveries aside, I mean."

Surprisingly, Stirling was the first to respond. He filled me in on the renovations he and Mikey were doing to his place. Mikey had moved in with him a few months back.

He had changed so much in the almost twelve months he had been with Mikey, and as someone who had known him for nearly twenty years, it was so good to see. He had come out of his shell. Mikey activated his protective and caring instincts, which allowed him to access parts of himself that he had never allowed himself to explore before. He was happier, lighter, and more talkative than I had ever seen him.

"What about you two?" I said, glancing over at Steel and Nick sitting beside me on the couch.

They both looked at each other, then Nick looked at me, back to Steel, then back at me. All the while, his mouth was pressed firmly shut.

Even though he was Mikey's best friend, I'd only really known the guy since he'd been with Steel, which was about six months. I did, however, know him well enough to realize that his mouth never stayed shut for this long. Was something up between them?

Before I could plunge into any further psychoanalysis, Steel finally spoke.

"We are good," he began, choosing his words carefully. "We're just at an... experimental stage of our relationship."

Porter's eyes lit up as they always did whenever the conversation took even the slightest detour into something sexual.

"Ooh, do tell," he said, rubbing his hands together in delight as he settled back into his chair.

"There's not much to tell," Nick said. "At least, not yet. But...I think...I think I might be a little."

The words were obviously hard for him to get out. He leaned into Steel's side, and Steel instinctively wrapped an arm around his shoulder.

"Hey, that's great, Nick," I said. "It's always fun and exciting to explore new parts of yourself."

"That's right," Porter added. Thankfully, that was *all* he added.

I was surprised at his restraint, but given how vulnerable Nick looked, I very much appreciated it.

The conversation turned light for a while, but I knew it was only a matter of time until the discussion swung back around to me. Rather than wait for it, I decided to bring up the topic of Liam myself.

"So I have some news," I said. They all turned to look at me. I grinned, planning to tease them for as long as I could. "You'll never guess who walked into the gym the other night."

My eyes practically popped out of my head as I was met with a chorus of Liam "I'm Always Right" Wrights.

What the hell?

"Wait, how did you guys know?" I said, my grin replaced with a grimace. They'd ruined all my fun.

"It's all over social media, Hudson," Mikey said. His bright blue eyes sparkled mischievously.

"It is blowing up like a big boy sitting on a cake," Nick threw in for good measure, back to his usual sassy self.

"Yeah, how many photos did you guys take?" Steel asked, looking at me. "It's literally all he's been posting for the last three days."

It was?

I wasn't a huge fan of social media and only ever logged on once a month or so. I pulled my phone out of my pocket, and with a few taps brought up Liam's social media accounts.

"Holy shit," I muttered under my breath as I scrolled down, looking at all the photos. The guys weren't pulling my leg, they were right. All of the images he had been posting over the last three days were...of us.

"Next time you see him," Porter said chortling, "ask him what Daddy filter he uses, because you look damn fine in those pics, Hudson."

I did?

I guess I didn't see myself the way that other people saw me.

I'd always been big and strong, that was how I got a weightlifting scholarship at Daylesford University. I never worked out to look good, it was a sport to me. The muscles were a byproduct, never the focus.

I got the ink stupidly young. I made some bad choices that I really regretted. It had taken me almost a decade, a shit ton of money, and countless hours in the chair to cover them up with the beautiful designs that I now had.

And my shaved head? That was more of a practical thing than anything else. Baldness was unfortunately hereditary in my family, and I started thinning out pretty badly in my late twenties. I didn't want to do comb overs, or hang onto the last strands of hair like a desperate man, so I took the plunge and shaved my head, Vin Diesel-style, a month before my thirtieth, and never looked back.

Nothing about my appearance was planned or staged. It certainly wasn't because I wanted to give off an alpha power-top vibe.

Why would I have wanted to do that, when it wasn't the truth of who I was?

"So what happened? What's the deal?" Steel asked.

"He just came into the gym and wanted a personal trainer," I said with a shrug, trying to make it sound light and spontaneous.

"How did *you* end up as his personal trainer?" Stirling asked, trying to hide the smile creeping along his lips.

Damn, these guys knew me too well. They knew I had stopped taking on new clients a few years ago.

They knew that the last new client I had taken on was...Richie.

"Hey, leave him alone, you guys." Porter was the last person I expected to come to my defense. "We all know he's been crushing on the guy for ages. This is good, Hudson is finally talking to the guy. And by the looks of Liam's social media, he seems kind of interested in our Hudson."

Was he interested?

I felt like an idiot for even asking him to help promote the gym, but he didn't seem to mind. And he didn't seem to waste too much time before asking for a favor of his own.

"What are you thinking?" Stirling asked, looking over at me.

I swallowed and suddenly wished we were at a bar, where I could find refuge in a vintage scotch.

"Well, uh...he did me a favor by promoting the gym, so I agreed to do him a favor as well."

Five sets of eyebrows shot up right away.

"What kind of favor?" Porter said as he leaned in.

"W—Well, he's got this event next week and he asked me to go as his...date. His *fake* date," I quickly added.

It wasn't real. It wasn't as if he liked me. It was me returning the favor.

A simple quid pro quo and nothing more.

So what if a part of me was more excited about it than I had been about anything else in a very long time? I was probably just happy to be leaving the house on a Friday night than anything else. Yeah, that was probably what it was.

"Just be careful with him, okay?" Porter said, and I could hear the genuine concern underpinning his words.

"What do you mean?" I asked.

"I've just heard a few things about him, that's all," Porter said.

"I have too, Hudson," Steel chimed in.

"Like what?" I asked. They'd never said any of this to me before.

"He's ambitious. He's ruthless. He's egotistical. He's a publicity whore that will literally go to the opening of an envelope..." Porter's voice trailed off.

I folded my arms across my chest. I didn't like listening to gossip or innuendo. Besides, I hadn't seen any of those traits that Porter had just listed. And I was a pretty damn good judge of character.

"So what's the event you guys are going to on your fake date?" Nick asked, making sure to stretch out his arms and use exaggerated air quotes around *fake date*.

"Uh..." Shit. This wasn't going to look good. "We're going to the opening of an envelope."

Porter threw his head back and let out a gratuitous *Ha!* while the others were more muted in their confusion.

"It's an exhibition," I added quickly. "An emerging artist has designed a series of envelopes and he'll be opening them on the night. It's a performance thing, a post-modern commentary on social interaction..."

My voice was sounding more desperate the longer I spoke.

It was a piece of pretentious horseshit and I knew it...but I didn't care if it meant a date with Liam Wright.

A fake date. A fake date with Liam Wright. I had to keep reminding myself to add that word.

"I'm just surprised," Steel said as he leaned back into the sofa. "I never had you pegged as being interested in art."

"Oh, yeah," I said, grateful that someone believed me. "I have been...for a while now. I mean, look, I'm sure this local artist is no Tchaikovsky, but I think it's important to support local emerging talent, you know?"

For some reason, the guys snickered at that remark.

"Just be careful, Hudson," Porter said once the snickering had stopped. "I know you've had a crush on him for forever, but this is a guy who's willing to do anything to get his face—or his ass—into the papers."

"Speaking of his ass," Nick piped up, "is it true that he gets booty shots? I mean, the guy is not a big boy like me, and yet, he's got an ass that I would kill for."

More laughing from the group, but not from me. I smiled and let it pass, but in some small way, it bothered me.

I knew there was more to Liam Wright than just his ass and a cute catchphrase. I hadn't been lying to him when I said his ass was my eighteenth favorite thing about him. Sure, I didn't have a complete list of all the things I liked about him...yet...but I wanted to.

Right now, I could easily add a few things to that list, like his adorable smile with that crooked tooth, how he was a hard worker at the gym and never gave up no matter how much his arms started to shake approaching the end of a set, and that he was even cuter in real life than he was on TV.

There, three out of eighteen wasn't a bad start, was it?

"It's nice that he's helping you promote the gym." How was it that Mikey was the voice of reason here? Normally it was me, but I was starting to get the impression he could be good in that role too.

"Thank you, Mikey," I said, flashing him a genuine smile. "It is very nice of him. Especially since you guys know how bad things with the gym have been lately."

"Is it still tough?" Steel asked with a pained expression on his face.

I nodded. "It is. And it's not getting better. Even after closing down the two suburban locations, it's still a struggle." I let out a heavy breath. "I've even been thinking about throwing in the towel and doing something else entirely."

I heard Nick gasp beside me.

"Like what?" Porter said, his brows pinched together tightly.

"I've actually been looking at going back to college to study psychology."

"Oh wow, you'd be great at that," Stirling said enthusiastically.

"Yeah, you definitely would," Steel said with an encouraging nod.

I even heard a quiet, but firm, *deffers* from Nick.

"Well, if there's anything we can do to help..." Porter said.

"Oh, believe me, you have. You alone, Porter, have given me twenty years of material," I said joyfully as the guys erupted in laughter around me.

Porter gave me the finger and steered the conversation in another direction. His.

I sank back into the chair, feeling relieved. I'd survived telling them about Liam. Even though they had some slight reservations about him, I didn't. I knew he was a good guy.

And I'd told them about possibly closing the gym so that I could go back to school. Well, I'd told them I was thinking of studying psychology at least.

There was another thing I had been studying for the last year and a half, but there was no way in the world I was going to tell them about that.

CHAPTER SIX

LIAM

"Holy sweet Jesus, mother of motherfucking fuckballs, he is hot," Parker said, fanning himself down as he scrolled through my social media feed.

"So you approve then?" I said with a laugh.

"I one thousand percent approve. This is genius, Liam."

"How so?" I asked, turning to face the mirror in my dressing room as I adjusted my hair.

I just couldn't seem to get the almost-but-not-quite three and a half inches to sit right. It kept flopping down, but I'd be damned if I was going to use hairspray to lift it back up. I ran my fingers through it, and settled on a raised, messy look.

It was an art exhibition after all, not the local media awards.

"Well," Parker began. "You look the way you do. Sweet, innocent, boy next door, disproportionately huge ass. That's you, that's your brand."

I rolled my eyes, but he either didn't see it, or he simply chose to ignore it.

"Whereas this slab of man meat...does he have a name?"

I scoffed. "Of course he has a name. Everyone has a name, Parker."

"Well, what is it?" he said testily. "It's not something boring or nerdy, is it?"

"You mean like *Parker*?" I joked.

"Parker is strong, sharp, and conveys both intelligence and good social standing."

"Let me guess, the testing told you that?"

He scrunched up his nose at me and tapped his fingers against his arm.

"His name, Liam?"

"His name is Hudson," I said, turning to put my coat on.

"Fucking perfect," Parker said, his face overtaken by a wide smile. "So you're *you*...and he's this big, tattooed brickhouse of muscle. The bad boy. The alpha. The powertop. Hudson."

He pretended to be swept off his feet as he said his name and fell into the empty chair.

"You're making a lot of assumptions there," I said, straightening my coat and taking a final look at myself in the mirror.

"I am," Parker said. "And with any luck, all of Daylesford will be making the same assumptions as well. Now before you go..." He got to his feet as he walked me to the door. "It would be really, really good if we got a kiss in front of the cameras."

"Uh, Parker, I don't know..."

"Not just for Mrs. Langley," he interrupted. "But for the promotion."

"You think it will really make a difference?" I still wasn't convinced.

Parker placed his hands on my shoulders and said definitively, "Yes, it will help you. Trust me. I mean, if I could kiss him for you, I totally would."

I half smiled. "You really think he's that hot?"

"Let me put it to you like this: I am a total top. Always have been, always will be. But I would bottom so hard, as if my life depended on it, for that man. He is that fucking hot."

Well, that was quite the ringing endorsement.

"Anyway," Parker said, straightening his shoulders. "The limo is downstairs and waiting, so go on, scoot."

"You ordered a limousine?" I asked, shaking my head.

"Hey, if you want to be a superstar, you gotta look the part."

I kept my face blank as I said goodbye, not wanting to give him the satisfaction of being right.

Twenty minutes later, the limousine pulled up in front of a nice-looking house in one of Daylesford's most exclusive suburbs. The door opened before I could get out, and Hudson, all six-foot-six of him, got into the limo beside me.

"Hey," I said excitedly. The sight of him instantly perked me up and managed to drown out all of Parker's well-intentioned advice, which was still running through my mind. "You look great."

He did. He was wearing dark denim jeans, a crisp white shirt that clung to his chest and pecs wickedly, a smart navy blazer, and a pair of black leather shoes.

"Thanks," Hudson said casually, but a smile tugged at the edges of his lips. "You don't look so bad yourself."

The man looked good in workout gear, but sporting this smart casual look, I could certainly see what got Parker so worked up and considering becoming a switch. Hudson might have been one of the few men who actually looked better with more clothes on.

Although, would it be so bad to see him with all his clothes...off?

As the driver pulled away, I grabbed the small handheld mirror from the backseat and fussed with my hair again. It did need to be up. That was what the studio wanted. It was what the testing had revealed to be most popular.

"Are you okay?" Hudson asked, picking up on my agitation.

If it were up to me, I'd shave my whole damn head like he had. I really wasn't into superficial things like the length of my freaking hair, but I knew it had to be done. It only mattered to me because it would help me get that promotion.

"Hey, hey, hey," Hudson said as he gently grabbed my arm to stop me from picking at my hair like a deranged seagull. "What's the matter, Liam?"

I threw the mirror away. I couldn't believe it, but I was fighting back tears.

"Your hair looks fine," Hudson said, his green eyes wide and sincere. "You look amazing just the way you are."

I ignored the fluttering in my heart and looked at him.

"It needs to be higher," I said, not liking the petulant quality in my voice. "Testing says it needs to be higher."

"Testing?" he asked. His brows arched as he studied my face intensely.

"Focus groups, you know?" He nodded, but still looked as confused and concerned as before. "Plus it's in my contract. It's in everyone's contract. All on-air male talent have to have a hair length between three and five inches. We even have a production meeting every Monday to measure our hair."

"You do?" he asked. There was curiosity in the way he said it, but no judgment.

I nodded as I let out a deep sigh and turned to face him. "When was the last time you saw a guy on the news that didn't have amazing three-to-five-inch hair?"

Why was I telling him all of this? What was I expecting him to do?

"Hmpf," he said as he scuttled toward me. "I guess you're right. I've never even thought about it before. Good thing a career in the media never interested me."

He kept getting closer until his thigh pressed against mine. What was he doing?

"Well, if we need to get you looking a certain way..." He ran his thick fingers through my hair, holding it up in place. "Then let's get you looking a certain way."

Relief washed over me as I looked into his eyes. Relief mixed with...something else.

"But just between you and me," he said, continuing to play with my hair. "I think you look kind of perfect just as you are."

A warm feeling flooded my insides.

"There," he said after a few moments of styling. He grabbed the mirror that I had thrown away, and handed it to me. "Better?"

I looked at my reflection and had to blink twice. He had done it. Somehow he had made my stubbornly uncooperative hair manage to stay up and look...good. Damn good.

"Thank you," I said as I placed my hand on his lap.

He lifted my hand up to his mouth and gave it a gentle kiss. It didn't stop the fiercest of searing heats shooting through my entire body. Then his eyes widened and he quickly returned my hand to my lap.

"I'm sorry, I shouldn't have done that," he said, clearing his throat and looking straight ahead.

"No, it was great," I said.

He turned to look at me.

"It was?" he asked.

I was shocked at the softness in his voice and the gentleness of his face. Especially considering that he looked like the kind of guy who wouldn't hesitate to snap someone in two if they so much as looked at him the wrong way.

"Yes," I said with a nod. "It adds to the believability. I mean, we are trying to pretend that we're on a date, right?"

For a moment, he looked crushed. But then that look—whatever it was—disappeared.

"Good," he said, clearing his throat. "That's exactly what I was going for."

I let out a chuckle. "It's funny, because my publicist actually wanted us to kiss on the red carpet."

"She did?" Hudson said.

"*He* did, yes," I corrected. "But I said no."

"Oh. Why's that?"

"Well, I just felt bad," I explained. "I didn't want you to feel like I was just using you. I'm—I'm not the kind of guy that would do that to anyone."

Again, why was I telling him this?

"I can tell you're not," Hudson said, and suddenly, his fingers were interlaced with mine.

"How?" I asked, studying the man. Why did he, a complete stranger, think he knew me so well?

"I don't know," Hudson said, and I could feel his fingers wanting to pull away, but they didn't. "Don't hate me for this, but I'm kind of, like, one of your, like, biggest fans ever." He rolled his eyes. "Sorry, that sounded so pathetic."

I let out a soft laugh. "It's not pathetic at all."

It wasn't.

It was cute, not creepy. I could tell he wasn't just interested in me because I was on TV, or said some stupid catchphrase, or had a huge ass. He seemed to really like me for me, and that felt really good.

My phone vibrated in my pocket, so I quickly grabbed it. Maybe it was Parker texting with some last-minute advice. It *was* a text from Parker, but it wasn't advice. It was an announcement.

I had won the *Daylesford's Hottest Derriere* award.

"What is it?" Hudson asked, his grip tightening around my fingers in the yummiest of ways.

I showed him the text and he smiled.

"Congratulations," he said. "Wait, why aren't you happy? I thought you said this was what you wanted? You were a shoo-in, remember?"

I did remember saying that to him at my first personal training session. And I also remembered feeling like a complete douchebag afterward.

"Can I be honest with you for a minute?" I said, looking away from his eyes, which never seemed to leave my face.

"Of course," he said.

I could feel him brushing the back of my hand with his thumb, and it felt reassuring.

"I don't like any of it. The stupid catchphrase. The stupid publicity I'm always seeking. The stupid tight pants I'm always wearing. It's all just so..."

"Stupid," he offered. I looked up at him; his eyes were round and soft.

We both smiled.

"Yeah," I finally said. "I just want to do the weather and maybe one day...ah, forget it. It's stu—it's nothing."

"Tell me," he said in a tone that made me want to obey him.

"I really care about the environment. Now, before you say anything, I know it's boring and negative and depressing and no one wants to hear about it, but...I care. I don't think it's any of those things, I think there's a really good chance that we can all make a difference. I'll stop talking now."

Hudson's fingers slipped away from mine.

I knew it, Parker was right. Talking about this sort of stuff turned people off big time.

The next thing I knew, his fingers were grazing my jawline.

"I don't want you to stop talking, Liam," he said in that hypnotizing voice of his. It was a blend of deep, warm, and sexy.

"You don't?" I asked.

He shook his head. "No, I don't. You sometimes give hints when you're on the air about this sort of stuff. You mention some cool climate facts, or that there's a rally happening somewhere. It's not a lot but it's just these little bits every once in a while. And I like that. I like that you care, that there's more to you than all of that superficial stuff. As I said to you before, your ass is my eighteenth favorite thing about you."

Hudson rested his fingers under my chin. I couldn't help but stare into his friendly eyes. He cocked his head at the same time as I tilted mine. I could feel his fingers wrapping around mine again, pressing firmly. Our heads moved toward one another until I could smell the spicy warmth of his cologne. I leaned in further and began to close my eyes...

"We're here, Mr. Wright," the driver said, winding down the internal window. Hudson jumped a mile.

"Right," I said, clearing my throat. "Thank you for that."

I looked over at Hudson. His face was blank and his body was still, except for his thumb which was racing up and down against his fingers in the clenched fist he was making.

"Are you ready to do this?" I asked.

"Sure," he said, looking straight ahead. "I mean, how hard can a local red carpet be?"

CHAPTER SEVEN

HUDSON

The first thing that struck me when the limousine door was opened was the wall of sound that hit us. It was like being sucker punched in the face, but somehow, I managed to scramble out of the car—with a little dignity, I hoped—and hold my hand out for Liam.

If I thought it was loud before, the second he got out of the limo, the volume dial got turned all the way to extreme. There were fans screaming his name, cameras flashing, bright lights, and fast-moving people whirring all around. And the noise, it was...inescapable. It felt like it was coming from everywhere.

Liam, of course, was a consummate professional. He fixed a wide smile onto his face and squared off his shoulders. A part of me was beaming with happiness that I was his date for the night.

His fake date.

But another part of me couldn't help but wonder what would have happened if we weren't interrupted in the limousine. Would we have actually kissed? Because that part didn't feel fake, at least not for me.

Suddenly, Porter's voice came into my head, and it was never a good thing when that happened. As I looked at Liam, the concerns that Porter and Steel had raised echoed in my mind.

The guy was a professional. He was in the media, so yeah, this probably was what he'd said it would be. A fake date. Nothing more and nothing less.

He was more interested in believability, and making Mrs. Langley happy, than he was in me. I just had to accept that. Which was why I was surprised to feel his fingers slip into my hand as he walked up the red carpet, half a step in front of me.

Believability, I reminded myself. He was just doing it to make it seem to the world like he was on a real date.

I was so busy looking at the chaotic scene around us that I almost crashed into him when he suddenly stopped and started posing for the cameras.

"Liam, who's your date tonight?"

"Liam, what piece are you looking forward to seeing tonight?"

"Liam, how do you feel about winning Daylesford's Hottest Derriere?"

I gently slipped my fingers out of his hand, cupped my hands together behind my back and moved a few steps away. The shouting pack of hyenas were interested in him and not me.

He was standing there, silent but smiling widely. For a moment, despite his outward appearance of poise and happiness, I saw the faintest glimmer of sadness. There was a certain vulture-like quality to the scene I was witnesing when I saw it up close and personal, standing there on the red carpet like I was.

He was just one man, silhouetted against a pack of hungry, rapacious, and roaring vultures. The questions kept flying at him and he kept on ignoring them. His smile remained plastered on his face, and as he turned from side to side, the cameras moved with him. It felt a little voyeuristic, predatory, and just...sad.

I'd always felt like there was more to him than just being Daylesford's hottest weatherman, with what was now, officially, Daylesford's hottest ass. But it was always just a feeling, something that I put down to simply having a crush on the guy.

But now I knew there *was* more to him.

He had a deeper side. He cared about the environment and important issues. He wanted to make a difference in the world, a real difference. Yet here he was being paraded like a circus animal.

After a few moments, he turned to me. He motioned with his head for me to come back to him. I stepped up beside him as he whispered in my ear, his wide smile never faltering, not even for a second.

"Save me." His warm breath filled my ear. "Hold me, look happy for a moment, and then pull me away. Please."

"Okay," I whispered back to him. I stretched the biggest grin I could manage onto my face. "I got you."

I wrapped my arm around him and the camera bulbs exploded in a flurry of light. So did the questions coming from the voracious media pack.

"Liam, is this your new boyfriend?"

"Can you both turn to the left?"

"Liam, what's the weather for tomorrow? I forgot to watch the news."

The questions kept coming, but I figured since he wasn't responding, we just had to stand there, pretend we couldn't hear them, and take it.

Liam slipped his hand back into mine. I could feel him shivering, so I rubbed the back of his hand with my thumb to reassure him and calm him down a little. It seemed to work. Within a few moments, the shivering had completely gone.

I was just about to pull him away, when one of the reporter's questions stopped me dead in my tracks. It rang out above all the other questions that were being hurled at us.

"Liam, is it true you're moving to New York to join Wake Up America?"

What was that about? Was Liam really planning on leaving Daylesford, or was it just another stupid rumor that I shouldn't believe?

I certainly felt like a deer in headlights, well more than I was already feeling that anyway. It was Liam's gentle touch—he was now stroking the back of my hand with his thumb—that brought me back to the red carpet.

"We're almost done," he said to me, and I was impressed at his ventriloquist skills. His lips barely moved, but he was as clear as day.

"Show us your ass."

"Yeah, turn around and show us your ass."

The vultures were turning feral.

I felt Liam's grip on my hand get firmer, and as I turned to look at him, I could see his jaw was clenched as well.

He clearly hated this, being reduced to turning around and showing off his ass. I could tell that it was really pissing him off. I thought the reporters would back off, since they weren't getting Liam to turn around, but no, they intensified their calls.

"Liam, turn around."

"We need an ass pic."

"Do it, Liam, turn around."

My blood was starting to boil and I could see Liam begin to lose his composure a little. As the cries rang out louder around us, we looked at each other. I didn't know what came over me, but in that moment I knew that it was the right thing to do.

I grabbed Liam, swung him around so he was draped across the front of my body, tilted my head, and leaned in for a kiss. Liam's lips met mine and the touch felt electric, just as good as his body felt in my arms.

The shouting stopped and the reporters were reduced to

silence. All I could hear was the sounds of the cameras flashing, but soon, they faded away as well.

It was a soft kiss on the lips. I mean, we had to keep things PG. But it was long enough that when I finally lifted him back up to standing, his taste still lingered.

"How was that for believability?" I said, taking his hand and walking up the rest of the red carpet, with Liam half a step behind me.

The next morning, I didn't even get the chance to look up when Liam walked through the front doors of the gym. He ran up to the front desk and threw all of Daylesford's newspapers in front of me.

"What's all this?" I said, looking up and seeing him beaming at me.

His dark gray eyes were sparkling like I had never seen them sparkle before. He was practically buzzing with excitement.

"Look at these," he said, pointing to all of the newspapers now scattered across my front desk.

I picked one up.

"Holy shit," I said, looking up at him.

He was nodding his head manically.

"We're on the front cover of *The Daylesford Times*."

I couldn't believe it.

"Not just *The Daylesford Times*. All of them, Hudson," Liam said as he flicked his fingers across the newspapers.

I looked down, and he was right. We were on the cover of all of the newspapers in Daylesford, and the photo they had all used was of our kiss on the red carpet.

The image was the same on all the covers, or a slight variation of the same, depending on where the photographer had been standing. The only difference was in the headlines.

"Today's Forecast is for Hot and Steamy"

"Daylesford's Hottest Derriere...*and Hottest Kiss*"

"*Liam Wright's Hunky New Beau is Totally Right*"

"I take it by your smile that this is a good thing?" I asked with a chuckle.

"Are you kidding me?" he said, slamming his hands onto the counter. "This is fantastic, Hudson. Way better than anything I could have expected. Thank you so much."

The sparkle in his eye was gone, replaced by something more serious, more genuine.

"I'm glad I could help," I said as I began to scoop the newspapers up into a pile. "Are you ready for your workout this morning?"

I saw Liam suck in a breath as he slid his hands slowly off the countertop.

"Yeah, I kinda don't want to do that anymore," he said.

"Oh."

For some reason, it was a struggle to get that one syllable out.

"Yeah, I'm sorry. I don't really think I am a gym person. Nothing personal, at all. You were amazing," he added hurriedly, but not in time to stop my stomach from dropping to the floor. "With everything going on right now, I just don't have the time to give it the proper focus and attention I need to. I hope you can understand, Hudson?"

"Sure," I said, handing him the pile of neatly folded newspapers and ignoring the nervousness I must have imagined in his tone.

Porter's words started to make sense, and I hated it when that happened. Liam had gotten what he wanted. Publicity. I had just been too blind to see it, and too stupid to realize that I was simply a means to an end.

Liam cleared his throat, drawing my attention back to him. "My publicist called this morning and said that the network was really happy with the coverage too."

"That's great," I said. I was happy for him, and desperately trying to quash the disappointment that wanted to burst out of me.

I braced myself for the inevitable *thanks a lot and goodbye* I could tell was coming. Maybe it was better this way. Liam had gotten what he wanted and so had I. The gym had apparently received a lot of new inquiries since Liam had begun posting about us all over his social media.

And I got to have at least one fake date with my real crush.

All in all, it wasn't a bad ending for anyone. So why did I suddenly feel like crawling under the covers and watching *Romy and Michele's High School Reunion* on repeat for the rest of the day?

"I had a good time with you, Hudson," Liam said in a tone I couldn't recognize. It wasn't his TV voice, that was for sure. "And the kiss on the red carpet was great and all, but can I tell you something?"

I leaned in closer.

"What?"

Liam leaned in closer too.

"I kinda wish our first kiss had been in the back of the limo."

We both smiled and my heart throbbed heavily against my chest.

"But that kiss wouldn't have gotten us on the front cover of all of these newspapers," I said with a grin.

"Who cares?"

Liam kept leaning in, getting closer and closer to me. I wanted so badly to reach out and touch his soft face again. But I didn't. He was just being polite.

I kept reminding myself that a *thank you and goodbye* was coming up.

"Can I ask you a favor? Another one, that is."

Anything. I would literally agree to anything he asked me right at that moment.

"Sure," I managed to wheeze.

"Any chance we could turn our fake date into something more...semi-permanent?"

I grabbed my water bottle and gulped thirstily.

"What do you mean?" I asked.

"Would you like to be my fake boyfriend?" Liam asked, batting his eyelashes at me in the most criminally cute way two sets of eyelashes had ever been batted.

I was stunned silent.

"For Mrs. Langley, that is..." he added as a smile gently stretched across his lips.

"Sure," I said, drinking the remaining water in my bottle. "For Mrs. Langley."

CHAPTER EIGHT

LIAM

"This is good, this is good, this is good," Parker said as he furiously paced up and down my dressing room.

"Parker, stop it," I said.

He was making me nervous. "You know I don't like when you walk around like that. Stop it. It's freaking me out."

I heard him grumble something under his breath, but he came over and sat down across from me anyway.

It was kind of a big deal, asking Hudson to be my fake boyfriend. After his initial shock, which probably had more to do with the fact that he hadn't come up with the idea himself, Parker was totally on board.

It was, however, his idea to have this meeting with Hudson.

It would be a chance for the two of them to meet, and for the three of us to figure out some of the more practical things. Like how the hell this whole situation would play out, and what we had to do to make it feel as real as possible. Because, while a fake relationship was a good tactic to get a promotion, getting busted having a fake relationship was a surefire way of blowing those chances to smithereens.

"We haven't vetted him," Parker said, taking off his glasses and giving me his most serious of serious looks.

I burst out laughing.

"Parker, he's going to be the fake boyfriend of a local weatherman. He's not a candidate for vice president of the country, for god's sake. We don't need to do a complete background check on the guy."

Parker was unimpressed. He proceeded to put his glasses back on and started combing through the papers on his ever-present clipboard, which was basically an extension of his body at this point.

"Well, if we're not going to run a proper background check on the guy, let's just go over what you do know about him, shall we?" He peered up at me through his glasses.

"Sure," I said, injecting as much confidence into my voice as someone who had no idea who Hudson really was could possibly inject. What I didn't know in specific details, was more than made up for with the gut feeling I had about the man.

He may have been a fan, and that may have rung an internal alarm bell when he first said it, but he quickly proved he was no ordinary, run-of-the-mill fan who just wanted a quick selfie, or for me to say the damn catchphrase.

I didn't know how he did it, but he made me feel safe when I was with him. Which surprised me, because frankly, I didn't think I was the kind of person that felt unsafe. Yet, whenever he was around, I just felt better with him there.

And I meant what I had told him at the gym, I *did* wish our first kiss had been in the back of the limo. Even though it would have been breaking the rules, and been more real than fake, it would have been nice to have just a little something that was real in my life.

But the kiss on the red carpet had felt pretty damn real too. I mean, sure, there were photographers snapping away all around us, but it was the fact that *he* did it. Not me.

I think he sensed how uncomfortable I was getting, so it was probably just that. He wanted to do something to distract the reporters from my ass. So he kissed me. I'm sure it wasn't anything more than that.

He did this funny thing where he asked me questions, though. For someone who had questions shouted at him on the red carpet, or asked in sit-down, faux-serious interviews by faux-serious local reporters, I found his questions disarming.

It was like he was trying to get to know me better. The real me, not the *Liam "I'm Always Right" Wright* me.

The public me wasn't a completely different version of who I was, but it was, in some ways, a character that I played. I took some parts of the real me, and magnified the good bits that would test well with focus groups, while reducing the parts that viewers wouldn't like.

Like serious opinions about the environment, for instance.

He also did a really weird thing after he asked me a question.

He listened.

Like, really listened to what I was saying. That was unnerving, because I wasn't really used to people listening to what I had to say. Not that I ever really got the chance to say anything controversial, or deep, or even...real.

I was rapidly discovering that I might have been a good meteorologist, and good at getting media attention and publicity, but I kinda sucked at the whole *being a normal person* thing. I was definitely more of a human *doing* then a human *being*.

I'd never had anyone genuinely interested in me before. I'd never even had anything close to a relationship before. I had this weird wall around me. I didn't know where it came from, but it was always there. It meant that I was okay with not having people get too close to me. It was a part of me that felt wrong and broken, and that I would have to fix some day.

But right now, all I wanted was to focus on my career, and for that, I had to be all in. Getting this promotion and joining *Wake Up America* was my singular focus. It had to be. I couldn't get distracted by...

"What is Hudson's surname?" Parker's question hit me like a torpedo.

"Uh...Madden," I replied. I remembered it from the paperwork I had signed when I'd joined the gym.

"How old is he?"

Wow, okay, Parker was taking this seriously.

"Forties-ish," I replied, hoping my bright smile would cover my lack of knowledge.

"Liam, you know your smiley, cutesy shit doesn't work on me. I'll leave that one blank," Parker said, returning to his clipboard and scribbling away furiously. "We know what he does for a living, and we know he's single, right?"

"Yep," I said with a firm nod. "I asked him point blank, and he said he was."

"Oh, that's so good," Parker said, speaking with an exaggerated saccharine sweetness as he clutched dramatically at his chest. "Because no man in the history of humankind has ever lied about whether he was single or not."

I let out an agitated groan. "Why would he lie, Parker? He's the one doing me a favor, remember? It's not like being my fake boyfriend was his lifelong ambition and I'm giving him his one shot at it."

"Okay, okay, point taken," Parker said, readjusting himself in his seat.

"And be nice to him when he gets here, okay?" I said, shooting Parker a pointed look.

"What do you mean?" he asked, his voice going up an octave. "I'm always nice."

I let that one go without any further comment.

"I just mean," I began, "he's not from this crazy world of ours. He's just a regular guy doing me a favor. Please promise me that you will remember that, and not say or do anything to make him uncomfortable."

"Fine, I promise," Parker murmured.

Before I could press him further to make sure that he meant it, there was a knock on the door. Parker shot up out of his seat to open it.

"Well hello, Mr. Madden," he said, overly loudly—and sweetly.

I grumbled to myself. Of course his attempts to make Hudson feel comfortable would also be designed to make me uncomfortable. The cheeky shit.

Parker and Hudson shook hands in the doorway before Hudson stepped into my dressing room.

And wow, did the man look good.

I'd seen him in his training clothes, as well as in a smart casual getup for our fake date, but I'd never just seen him wearing normal clothes. Although there was nothing normal about the way his clothes clung to his beastly frame. It was just a gray shirt and a pair of light jeans, but damn, the man looked like he was dripping sex.

He saw me and smiled, making my heart skip faster. I grinned like an idiot right back at him.

"Hey," he said.

"Hey," I replied.

What were we supposed to do? Shake hands? Hug? Have him drape me over his body and lean him in for a kiss again? I would have been happy with option three.

"Please have a seat, Mr. Madden," Parker said politely as he looked at the two of us standing frozen in front of one another.

"Can I get you something to drink, Mr. Madden? Coffee? Tea? Water? Vodka?"

"Call me Hudson, please," he said as we moved over to the couch.

We sat down at the same time. Our knees touched briefly and I felt warmth spread throughout my entire body. What the hell was that?

"And no, nothing for me, thanks," he said, looking over at Parker, who was pouring himself a generous vodka with a splash of tonic.

"Okay, well thank you for coming," Parker said, sitting down across from us.

The ice cubes in his drink jangled loudly and I couldn't help but giggle quietly to myself. This was all so surreal.

Parker, to his credit and despite drinking at what was essentially a business meeting, kicked into professional mode. He explained the arrangement to Hudson in simple terms.

He and I were becoming fake boyfriends, so we needed to do some real boyfriend stuff. Like dinner at a restaurant. Like a few selfies snapped at each other's houses. Like a few changes to our social media accounts' relationship status. Like not being seen out in public with anyone else.

"Do you have a problem with any of that?" Parker asked once he was done explaining.

"No, it all sounds good to me," Hudson said, and sent a casual smile my way.

Why hadn't Parker offered me a drink? I could have done with one right about now.

"And you definitely are single, right?"

"Parker," I snapped. "Don't be rude."

"I'm not being rude," Parker huffed back. "I'm sorry if I offended you, Hudson, but I need to ask."

"It's totally fine," Hudson brushed it off with a rich, deep laugh that instantly calmed me down.

"I understand you have a job to do, Parker, and I respect that. And yes, I am definitely single."

I understood how tornadoes formed in the Pacific and made their way up the coast. I knew how clouds banded together to form lightning. But explaining how this man was still single, well, that defied any logic or reason.

He was smart, successful, funny, thoughtful, and insanely attractive...why *was* he single?

He hadn't given me even the slightest clue during any of our interactions up until that point. He didn't really talk much about himself at all. In fact, he was always the one asking me questions.

Right at that moment, I decided that I would use our upcoming fake dates to try and get at least a little bit of information out of Hudson Madden.

I wasn't interested in the specifics of his life the way that Parker was. This wasn't about backgrounding the man, it was about getting to know him and who he was a little more. After all, even if we were only going to be fake boyfriends, it couldn't hurt to know a little bit about each other.

For believability, that is.

"The most important thing to remember, guys," Parker said, carefully placing his drink down onto the coffee table, "is to take photos and selfies of everything. It's like a tree falling in the woods. If you don't photograph it, did it really even happen?"

Hudson chuckled.

I liked watching his whole chest vibrate when he laughed. For a second, I wondered what it would feel like to run my hands over that massive chest.

I cleared my throat and turned my attention back to Parker.

"Uh huh, that makes sense," I said.

"You'll have to take most of the photos though," Hudson said, gently placing his hand on my knee. The rush of heat at his touch was instant.

"Oh, yeah?" I said, turning to look into his gleaming green eyes.

"Yeah, I suck at selfies and all that social media stuff. Sorry."

There was something about seeing this giant beast of a man apologizing for something he didn't need to apologize for that was so captivatingly charming.

"It's alright," I said, putting my hand over his. "I can take care of all of that stuff."

We looked at each other for a moment, before I could feel Parker's gaze burning a hole through the side of my head.

"That's great then," Parker said, lifting his drink off the coffee table and bringing it to his lips. "Are you both free this Saturday night?"

We both nodded.

"Good," Parker said. "I'll book the best table at Montrachet for eight."

"I love French food," Hudson said, turning to me with a wide smile.

"Same," I said, looking back at him and trying to not get lost in those dazzling eyes of his.

He didn't look away. His gaze met mine firmly.

It sparked a yearning low in my belly. The longer he looked at me like that, the more I never wanted him to stop looking at me.

What was he doing to me?

I was only reminded that Parker was still in the room when he cleared his throat emphatically.

"I will also call all of my paparazzi contacts to let them know that you guys will be there..."

"Uh huh..." I said, not willing to turn away from Hudson, and not ready to think about anything else. I was basking in the warmth of those light green eyes staring back at me.

"For your *fake* date," Parker said pointedly.

CHAPTER NINE

HUDSON

The plan was simple.

Meet in front of Daylesford's finest French restaurant, Montrachet, just before eight on Saturday. Parker had anonymously leaked to the local media that Liam Wright was going to be having a hot date with his new beau there.

The paparazzi pack would be there, of course, waiting. We would show up separately, meeting in front of the restaurant, and right in front of the field of photographers, to give them what they were waiting for.

Parker suggested a gentle kiss on the cheek and maybe an embrace. He wanted to keep things sweet for Mrs. Langley. Either way, he left it up to me to decide. I was pretty sure I had heard him mutter something about me being a powertop alpha under his breath, but I didn't want to press him on it. I had probably misheard anyway.

I parked around the corner from the restaurant. Liam was going to park around the other corner, so that way we would be approaching the restaurant from opposite directions. Timing was crucial, so I quickly sent him a text.

Me: *Just pulled up. Let me know when you're ready.*

When I didn't hear back from him immediately, I figured he was still on his way and unable to text back. I tapped my fingertips on the steering wheel to drown out the thoughts racing through my head.

I still hadn't entirely figured out why I had agreed to this.

Meeting Liam and his publicist last week was meant to clear things up and make sure we were both on the same page. But I'd walked away from that meeting feeling more confused than ever.

It was weird to be in a fake relationship with someone who was a genuinely nice guy. I knew that he didn't want to be in a real relationship. Heck, the whole reason he was doing this was because he didn't have time for things like dating or having a boyfriend. I got that, I really did.

And I didn't know whether I wanted to be in a real relationship either. Some of it had to do with Richie. Even though I knew it had been almost four years, there was a part of me that still felt like it was unresolved. Like I hadn't found the closure that I needed.

But most of it, the bigger part of it, was to do with me. I wasn't sure whether I was ready to date someone for real. Because dating someone for real meant that you had to open up and be honest with them. And every time I had tried doing that with a guy, it had blown up in my face.

Even though we hadn't spoken about it, it was pretty clear that sex was not on the table for us. Parker said we needed to photograph everything we did, and there was no way Mrs. Langley would approve of anything X-rated.

Which was a good thing. Because the second I veered into sex territory, shit got weird.

I hated labels with a passion. Top, bottom. Daddy, boy. Dom, sub. They were just so...limiting.

What I liked, what I was into, wasn't covered by any of them. And for too many years, it had made me feel bad, as if there were something wrong with me because I didn't fit into a predetermined, cookie-cutter sexual label.

Even though things were slowly getting better and people were gradually becoming more open-minded and less...binary in their thinking, it was incredibly rare to find someone with the same tastes, interests, and preferences.

Maybe that was why I was feeling comfortable with what was happening with Liam.

In a way, I was more comfortable having a fake relationship with him than I would be having a real one. I got to hang out with him, which I really, *really* enjoyed. We were getting to know each other and he was just as incredible as I'd hoped he would be.

And we were having fun together. My internal fangirling had dropped by the wayside, so I could just hang out with him without it being weird.

He went from being my crush to being my fake boyfriend...and that was enough for me.

It had to be.

My phone vibrated in my hand.

Liam: *Just got here. Sorry for the delay. My hair wasn't cooperating again.*

Me: *I'm sure you look amazing. Did you need me to sneak out and fix it up for you though? Haha...*

Liam: *Hehe, thanks, it's all good. Are you ready to do this?*

Me: *I am. Just popped a breath mint. Are you?*

Liam: *How considerate. Yep, let's go!*

And with that, I got out of the car and made my way around

the block to Montrachet. I rolled my shoulders down my back, adjusting them in the tight suit jacket I was wearing.

When I turned the corner and caught my first glimpse of Liam, my breath hitched in my throat. He looked absolutely divine. He was dressed in a slim-fitting gray suit with a black turtleneck underneath, highlighting his handsome features beautifully.

Our timing was perfect.

We met right in front of the elegantly lit restaurant entrance. There were a few photographers milling around, dressed in the unofficial paparazzi uniform of all black, and reeking of desperation and lack of moral compass.

"Hi," Liam said, outstretching his arms to me.

"Hi yourself," I said with a warmth filling me up from the inside. I placed one arm around his waist and gave him a gentle peck on the cheek. It was barely a graze, but I could have sworn I heard a tiny moan escape from his lips. Or maybe it was the sounds of the cameras flashing and clicking around us.

Yeah, it was probably that.

"After you," I said after our perfectly timed kiss.

Liam led the way into the restaurant and I followed close behind him.

Once inside, we were escorted to our table by the friendly-looking maitre d'.

"Oh," I said when we reached the table. It was beautifully appointed, but it was tucked away in the far corner of the restaurant, away from the front window.

"Is there a problem, sir?" she asked with an apprehensive smile.

"Is this table okay with you?" I asked Liam. "It's—it's quite far away from the *front*."

I was trying to be discreet and stay in fake-boyfriend mode.

"It's perfect," Liam said with a dismissive wave of his hand. Once we were seated and the maitre d' had handed me the wine menu, Liam leaned in closer and smiled. "I actually called the restaurant after Parker had made the reservation and requested this particular table."

"You did?" I almost dropped the wine menu onto the table. "Why?"

He leaned back and sucked his lower lip in between his teeth. "I know it's a fake date and all," he began. "But I just thought it would be nice if we could talk...for real. The photographers have what they want anyway, it's not like they're going to be eavesdropping on us all night. I thought this might be...nice. You know, give us a chance to get to know each other a bit?"

My heart started doing a happy dance in my chest.

"I'd love that," I said. I probably had the goofiest smile on my face, but I didn't care.

The only part of this entire fake relationship arrangement that I had been dreading was having to spend so much time together without it being real or sincere. A quick kiss for the cameras was fine, but spending an entire dinner in silence, or worse, only chitchatting about bullshit like the local sports team or the weath—well, maybe not the weather since I doubted that was a boring topic for him—didn't really appeal to me.

I liked Liam's idea...a lot.

He intrigued me and I couldn't wait to learn more about him. Once we had ordered our meals—confit of ocean trout, creamed beets, grilled polenta, green peas, and a dozen freshly shucked Pacific oysters for the appetizer, which he suggested we share, and a duck and cognac parfait for his entrée and a beef bourguignon for me, paired with the server's wine recommendations— I was ready to fire away some questions.

Before I had the chance, though, a question came flying straight at me.

"So," he asked with a devilish glimmer in his eye. "I've been meaning to ask you this since the first day I saw you, and I don't mean this in an objectifying way, but...how on earth did you get the body that you have?"

I let out a flat chuckle.

"Oh, you mean this thing?" I said, looking down at my chest. "I picked it up on Amazon. Got it for a good price too."

He laughed and quickly covered his mouth, as if he were worried it would be too loud.

"Actually, I've always been big. I was six feet tall by the time I was twelve."

I paused as the server returned with our wine.

"That is big," Liam said as we clinked our glasses together.

"I was always super into sports as a kid."

"Any sports in particular?" he asked. "Mmm, this wine is good."

I tasted it too.

"Yes, it's very good," I agreed. "I liked all sports. Hockey, basketball, football, tennis, you name it. But I was also strong, and I fell in love with weightlifting."

"Really?" Liam's eyebrows shot up, causing his forehead to crinkle delectably.

"Yes, really," I said with a nod. "I got really good at it actually. I made it to nationals when I was in high school. That's how I got into Daylesford University. It was on a sports scholarship for weightlifting."

"So what happened?" Liam asked, bringing the wine glass to his mouth. "I mean, why didn't you pursue it professionally after college?"

"The age-old issue. I hurt my lower back, pulled a disc. Pretty badly, actually. I completely ruptured the disc and had severe herniation of the nucleus through the annular wall."

"I don't know what any of those words mean, but they sound painful."

I could see Liam's gray eyes filled with worry.

"It all worked out for the best, though," I said, and for some reason my hand reached across the table to touch his. "I started Elite Fitness and have spent the last sixteen years building it up."

Even though now, it was falling down all around me.

Liam looked down at our hands, entwined on the table, but didn't say anything. I couldn't be sure, but I thought I did see a slight smile brighten his face.

"That's a huge achievement. It's really impressive," he said, looking up at me, his smile deepening.

"Yeah, well, I think I might be ready for something new," I said, taking a sip of wine.

"Have you got anything in mind?"

"I do, actually."

Liam looked at me expectantly.

"I guess my whole life has been about physical health, you know? Sports, weightlifting, the gyms. So I think I'd like to move into something that deals with mental health. I'm actually looking into studying psychology."

Liam's eyes widened.

"That's amazing," he said, squeezing my hand. "I am such a big believer in people following their passions. I love that you're doing that."

His youthful optimism was hard to resist.

"What about you?" I said, finally able to turn the conversation around and ask him my first question of the evening. "Are you following your passions?"

He was saved from answering by the appetizers arriving.

As soon as the server had gone, I pressed him again. "Well?"

For some reason, he was drawing it out. He grabbed a lemon and squeezed it over the oysters, before picking one up and throwing it back. He chewed it in his mouth for what felt like longer than it should have taken. Something was going on with him, I just had no clue what.

"I had a twin brother, Toby," he said eventually.

"Oh, I didn't know that," I said, surprised.

There was no mention of a brother on his Wikipedia page.

"He died when we were eight."

Liam looked away as my heart sank for him. The pain was

clearly evident in his voice. I couldn't even imagine what that kind of loss would have felt like, especially for a child at that age.

"I'm so sorry, Liam," I said, wanting to touch him again, but he had moved his hand back, his fingers resting on the edge of the table.

"No one knows," he said, looking at me.

"I won't tell anyone, I swear."

His eyes softened and he shot me a fragile smile.

"I know you won't," he said softly. "I trust you, Hudson."

I didn't know what to say, but he opened his mouth, ready to tell me the story.

"We used to be really outdoorsy kids," he began, and I remembered him starting off his story about why he got into weather in the same way. But this time, his voice was laced with a sincerity that I realized had been missing when he told me the story before.

"We were outside all day long, just playing and having fun. We'd get so tired that we'd lie on the grass and just look up at the sky, you know?"

I smiled a little, and he smiled back.

"We did that thing that all kids do. We'd look at the clouds and see all sorts of things in their random shapes. One cloud would look like the side of a house, another cloud would look like some sort of monster. That was my favorite thing to do with him, just lie on the grass and look up at the sky."

Liam took a heavy breath in.

"He died in a car accident with my grandpa. They both died. They were side-swiped by a drunk driver...at eight-thirty in the morning on their way to the park. It was horrible, for my mom especially. She lost her dad and her son in one day."

"I can't even imagine," I said.

"After Toby died, I'd lie on the grass by myself, looking up at the clouds like he and I used to."

Liam paused for a moment and I could tell he was choking back tears. He cleared his throat and, with a steadfast resolve, continued.

"Except, unlike before, I didn't see the shapes of familiar objects when I looked up at the clouds. There were no houses or monsters anymore. Instead...and I'll warn you, this is going to sound really weird..."

He looked over at me. I gave him a reassuring nod to let him know that whatever he said wouldn't be weird to me.

"It was like I could sense him in the shapes of the clouds. It was a feeling, more than anything else. So like, a dark cloud would mean he was trying to convey something sad, or a light and fluffy cloud would let me know that he was feeling happy, wherever he was. It made me feel like I still had him beside me in a way."

"That's not weird at all," I said, doing my best to talk around the lump that had formed in my throat. "It's really sweet, actually."

"I guess I spent so many hours just staring up at the sky, it made sense I would become fascinated with clouds and weather patterns. So, yeah, that's how I fell into meteorology, basically. That's why I'm so passionate about it, and about the environment. It's why I want to pass on that passion to future generations too."

Liam looked at me, his face suddenly flinching in surprise.

Then, slowly and without saying a word, he used the tip of his thumb to tenderly wipe away the single tear from the top of my cheek.

CHAPTER TEN

LIAM

It did something super crazy weird to my insides to see Hudson shed a tear for Toby like that.

It meant something to me that he was so affected by my story. He wasn't just a good listener, he was a compassionate one as well. And for a man that looked like a walking wall of muscle, it was nice to know that he was strong enough, and comfortable enough in his masculinity, to shed a tear.

The conversation remained light for the rest of the appetizers and well into the main course. The duck was decadently juicy and tender.

"You should really try this," I said with way too much duck in my mouth.

"Swapsies?" Hudson suggested with what looked like way too much beef in his mouth.

I managed to giggle without choking as we each put a forkful of food on the other's plate. Both dishes were exquisite and the night was going swimmingly...for a fake date, that is.

I had decided to take the lead in asking questions, wanting to know more about the gentle giant that sat across the table from me. I had started off strongly, but the detour into my childhood was unexpected.

I had never told anyone that story about Toby before. Not even Parker. I didn't know what made me tell Hudson. I knew that I could trust him, and it just felt like the right thing to say. Now that I had shared it with him, I was glad I did. I felt closer to him, which was a good thing to feel with your fake boyfriend.

"So," we both said at the same time and laughed. I guess we were both keen to keep the conversation going.

"Sorry, you go first," I said.

"No, you. Please," Hudson said with an affection in his voice that I couldn't ignore, or disobey.

"It's kind of personal," I said, wanting to give the man fair warning.

"I don't mind personal," he replied in a low grumble that sent a warm weather system spiralling up my spine. I wiped the sides of my mouth with the napkin and neatly folded it into a small square that I placed next to my now-empty plate.

"So, what's your love life history like?" I asked, grinning widely to mask the awkwardness I felt.

He chewed on the last remaining piece of food he had on his plate and then reached for the wine, before answering.

"I'm a little...hmm, I don't know what the word I'm looking for is, really," he said, and for the first time, I heard a hint of uncertainty in his voice.

"I've had relationships," he continued. "Even one serious one with...his name was Richie."

He paused and I wasn't sure what to do next.

He looked like he didn't know, either.

"But I guess dating has always been hard for me," he continued. I pinched my brows together, finding it more than a little hard to believe him. I studied his face for any signs of sarcasm, but his expression wasn't light. He was being serious.

"Do you mind if I ask why?" I said.

He looked up at me. His light eyes had turned a dark, mossy green.

He took another sip of wine, clearly trying to buy himself some more time as he figured out how to answer my question.

"I'm a little...unconventional."

"Oh," I said.

What the hell did that mean? Did I even want to know?

Not that I would have judged anything that came out of his mouth.

It was more that I worried that his experience in whatever unconventional things he liked, would completely dwarf my already limited *conventional* experience. A hurried handjob and a quick, sloppy blow job was my entire sexual resumé.

It was pathetic, at twenty-seven, to have had so little sexual experience, and for some reason, I didn't want him knowing the extent of my patheticness.

"How about you?" he said with a gentle cough. "How's your love life history?"

Great. If he was trying to make the conversation less awkward, he had just steered it in the completely wrong direction. I had to do a one-eighty, but how?

I looked at my empty plate and wine glass. I was completely out of reasons to delay my answer.

"I mean," Hudson asked, with that same uncertainty in his voice from before. "Have you ever dated an *older* guy?"

Older, younger, it didn't matter...the answer was still a straight-up no. But at least the way he had phrased the question gave me the slightest sliver of an out.

"No," I said, licking my dry lips with my dry tongue. "I've never dated an older guy before."

It was only as I was answering his question that I realized why he had asked it. It was clear as day, but somehow I had completely missed it.

He was older than me, quite a bit older, actually. Maybe the fake relationship didn't bother him, but my age did?

"Your turn," I said.

"Are you asking me if I've ever dated anyone older?" he said as a smug smirk spread across his lips. It made me want to reach right out and...kiss them.

"No, smarty pants," I said with a giggle. "Have you ever dated anyone younger?"

I wasn't expecting his response to be so quick and so...forceful.

"Exclusively."

The word hung in the air between us.

"So you've got no problem with me being younger than you?"

He smiled widely and licked his lips in an unintentionally seductive way.

"No problem at all."

I felt a flush run up my neck and into my cheeks. It was as if his words were burrowing their way into me. As if they were speaking to some deeper part of me. It made me feel unsure of myself.

"Why—why do you like younger guys?" I stammered.

Right at that moment, the server filled up our wine glasses. I practically dove at mine once it had been refilled.

This whole conversation, this whole evening was turning out to be so much more intimate than I had ever imagined. Funnily enough, it didn't bother me, and by the intent look on Hudson's face, it didn't seem to bother him either.

"As I said, there are many ways in which I'm not conventional. But I have always been attracted to younger guys, and as I've gotten older and more mature, throughout my thirties and now, having turned forty recently, I really enjoy being a Daddy."

A Daddy?

I tried my best not to squirm in my seat, but I must not have done a very good job of it.

"Are you okay?" Hudson asked, narrowing his eyes at me. "Is this conversation making you uncomfortable, Liam?"

I swirled the remaining wine around in my mouth before swallowing it and answering Hudson.

"No, I'm not uncomfortable," I said.

It was true. The topic of conversation wasn't making me uncomfortable. My complete lack of sexual experience, on the other hand, was. But that wasn't Hudson's fault. There was nothing he could do about that.

"It's just that, well, I'm definitely way more inexperienced than you are."

I managed to get the words out, hopefully without sounding like the biggest loser in the world. Hopefully.

"Oh."

Now it was Hudson who was looking uncomfortable.

"Would you like to keep talking? Or maybe we can change the topic and, you know, we can talk about something boring...like the weather."

I looked up to see him grinning from ear to ear.

"Ha, ha. Very funny," I said, grateful the tension had been broken, and very, *very* keen, to continue with the conversation, no matter how uncomfortable it was proving to be.

I wanted to know what he meant by being unconventional, but I also wanted to find out more about what being a Daddy meant to him.

"So," we both said at the same time, again, and laughed.

"You first, please."

His words were polite, but now I was picking up on a definite Daddy undertone. I tried to quiet my mind, so I could figure out what exactly it was that I wanted to find out from him.

"What does being a Daddy mean to you?" I finally asked.

"That's a really good question," he said, taking a sip of wine. "What I like about it is that it recognizes that there are many different ways to be a Daddy, just as there are many different ways to be a boy." He looked me straight in the eye. "Before I answer, can I ask you a question? Two, actually, if I may."

I nodded. "Yes, sure."

"Question one, how much do you know about Daddy/boy relationships?"

"Not a lot," I conceded with a shy smile.

"That's nothing to be embarrassed about," Hudson said tactfully. "I'm just asking so that I can calibrate my answer to wherever you are, I guess."

"Thanks."

"So in that case, you know that there's not just one way to have a Daddy/boy relationship? There's at least ninety-nine different ways. Well, way more actually, but ninety-nine sounds catchy, right?"

A small smile escaped my lips. "I do know that."

"Like any other type of relationship," Hudson continued, "a Daddy/boy relationship is as unique as the people involved."

I bit down on my tongue for a moment, mulling his words over in my mind, before I looked up and asked, "You said you had two questions for me?"

"I did, yes."

I couldn't tell whether knowing that Hudson was a Daddy was filtering how I was seeing him, but all of a sudden, every little gesture and movement the man made left me feeling lightheaded...in the best kind of way.

"Question two," he continued. "How honestly would you like me to answer your question?"

I let out a steady breath, and it felt like a huge weight had been lifted off my shoulders.

"Total honesty, please," I said. "Or whatever you're comfortable with."

He smiled, but his eyes were glazed over. I could tell he was mulling things over in his head, mentally deciding just how *honest*, honest really was. How much he really wanted to share with me. It was a lot to ask of him, I knew that. I was very keen to see how he would respond.

"I like to consider myself more of a teacher or a guide than a Daddy in the traditional sense of somebody who wants to control or dominate their boy. I guess one of the biggest differences is that I don't need to be called a Daddy, and I don't usually call my partner a boy. I have nothing against using those words, but for me, it's just not something that...I don't know, it just doesn't feel like it's right for me, you know?"

I nodded my head and smiled, wordlessly willing him to go on.

"For me, sex isn't just a physical thing. It's very much a form of communication. Something sacred and spiritual, but also something very ordinary and everyday."

I must have looked a little confused, because Hudson stopped for a second to smile as he scanned my face.

"What I mean is, instead of 'just fucking,' I tune in to whatever I'm feeling at that moment, whatever is going on for me—and my partner does the same—and then we use that as our starting point."

"Okay..."

"So, sex goes from being this thing where you go through the motions, step one through step come..."

I smiled and relaxed a little more.

I loved the way he was explaining this. It was the first time I'd ever had a conversation like this in my life, but it was feeling all sorts of right.

"...and instead, it's this new thing every time. If I'm feeling anxious about something, I might need more tenderness. If I'm angry, I might be rougher and more uncontrollable. Sometimes, I just need to be held, because it feels so damn good to be close to someone."

"So, it really is something different each time?" I asked as

Hudson tilted his head and nodded, looking happy that I was getting what he was saying.

"As a Daddy, I enjoy taking the lead in that process, but sometimes, that's not what's needed. Sometimes the boy, based on what he's going through, needs to take charge. And that's more than okay. Every time I have sex, it's like a brand-new spiritual and physical adventure."

He looked at me, his eyes scanning my face up and down, left to right. "Am I freaking you out with any of this?"

I shook my head fast.

"No," I said. "Believe me, no."

I knew a thing or two about freaking people out. You'd be surprised how quickly people moved away from you when you brought up two innocent-sounding words like, say, *climate change*.

I still didn't fully understand everything Hudson was saying, but it definitely wasn't freaking me out. If anything, it intrigued me. I wanted to know more.

I felt like what I already knew about the man was just the tip of the iceberg. He was passionate, smart, and caring. He was drop-dead gorgeous, a gentle giant underneath all of the muscles and tattoos.

And sexually, he was an unconventional Daddy.

A tide of desire rose within me, and before I knew what I was doing, I leaned over, tugged at his forearm, and pressed my lips into his. It was a soft kiss. We were in public, at a fancy restaurant, after all.

But I needed it.

I needed to feel the softness of his lips on mine, the earthy scent of him in my nostrils, and the touch of my fingers on his face. I pulled away and he opened his eyes slowly, like he was waking from a dream.

"I've wanted to do that ever since we were in the backseat of the limousine," I said. I was overcome with a feeling I'd never felt before. As I settled back into my chair, I realized what it was.

Desire.

"So, that was a real kiss then?" he asked.

I was struck by the vulnerability in the deep timbre of his voice.

"Yes," I said, observing him carefully. "That was a real kiss."

CHAPTER ELEVEN

LIAM

"I love it, I love it, I love it," Parker said, pacing up and down my dressing room with his head buried in the latest edition of *The Daylesford Times*.

"Can you please stop pacing?" I pleaded. "You know it makes me uncomfortable. Sit down and read it to me like a normal person."

Parked huffed loudly, but as always, came over and sat down across from me on the couch.

"Alright," he said, crossing his legs and resting the newspaper in his lap.

"We're the lead article on the social page, so that's a good start," he said, flashing me a bright smile.

"Headline?" I asked nervously.

Parker had been with me for about two years, but I still wasn't used to reading my own publicity. It was strange to be reading about yourself through the lens of a reporter who, in most cases, had never even met you, or if they had, had only spoken to you for a few brief moments.

"*Hot Night in the City for Daylesford's Hottest Weatherman,*" Parker read out loud, and then looked up at the ceiling, considering the words. With a firm nod, he looked at me. "Not bad," he said, still nodding. "The good thing is, the article's not too long, but the picture is huge. And you both look stunning."

"Show me."

He turned the paper around, and there we were. Hudson and I embracing in front of Montrachet. It all looked so romantic. So real. So totally the opposite of the staged, set-up photo op that it was. It looked so good that even my own heart fluttered a bit.

Parker was right about the article. It wasn't very long.

"What did they write?" I asked.

"Alright," Parker said, clearing his throat. "*KDR-nine weatherman Liam Wright...*" Parker looked up and winced. "Damn, they didn't use the catchphrase."

"They also didn't start off by saying *twenty-seven-year-old KDR-9 weatherman,*" I pointed out.

Parker's eyes widened. "You're right, good pickup."

He turned back down to continue reading. "*KDR-nine weatherman Liam Wright was spotted Saturday night about to step into one of Daylesford's most popular French restaurants, Montrachet.* That's good, should get me a free dinner there."

I rolled my eyes, while Parker scrunched his nose at me and kept on reading.

"*On the handsome, up-and-comer's arm was his rumored new boyfriend, forty-year-old owner of Elite Fitness Gym, Hudson Madden.*"

Parker paused for a second to look at me.

"*Up-and-comer* is good, right?" I asked as I bit down on my lower lip.

"*Up-and-comer* is *very* good," he said with a wide grin. "That's exactly how we want to be positioning you right now for this promotion. And for future reference, *up-and-comer* is always better than *down-and-goer*."

We giggled like two naughty school kids, before Parker continued.

"*According to a well-placed source*...which would be me..." Parker said, looking up. He always loved being the anonymous, well-placed source. "*...the couple are enjoying spending time together and getting to know each other better.* That's it. What do you think?"

After repeating it in my head a couple of times, I decided.

"I'm happy with it," I said. "Much better than the draft you suggested yesterday."

An unconvincing look of fake innocence crossed Parker's face.

"What was wrong with my first draft?" he asked. "Just because it was a little steamy..."

"A little?" I interrupted. "You were making it sound like Hudson was fucking me all over town."

Parker huffed and folded his arms across his chest.

"Don't give me that look," I said. "And you know Mrs. Langley would not have been happy with your X-rated draft."

He sighed loudly as I smiled. Mrs. Langley was the undisputed trump card of all trump cards, and we both knew it.

"Let's move on, shall we?" Parker said, throwing the newspaper onto the coffee table.

"Let's," I replied cheerfully.

"Testing has come back, and this new relationship thing is really working. I don't know what you're doing or how you're doing it, but your chemistry with Hudson is really coming through, especially for the fifty-plus demo."

Parker's eyes scanned the page intently.

"Also, straight guys between twenty-four and forty-five are responding well for some reason. It's probably because Hudson looks like *the dude they'd fuck if they had to fuck a dude*," Parker said, putting on his best dude voice.

I giggled. "Really? That's how the focus groups see Hudson?"

"Uh, yeah, hello, have you seen him?" Parker shot back. "Like I keep on telling you, I'm a total top, but I would totally bottom so hard for the guy. He could treat me like his bottom bitch any time he wanted to."

"Parker," I exclaimed. "Don't talk like that. It's so degrading."

"It's not degrading if it's well-communicated and consensual."

Parker's response surprised me. Given that the nature of our working relationship was mainly focused on me, I hadn't really gotten to know the guy on a personal level over the last two years.

"What about you?" I asked, narrowing my eyes at him. "You know, Parker, I don't know anything about your social life...or your sex life."

"Not much to tell, really," Parker said, standing up and walking over to the window. "My social life is my PlayStation."

He peered through the blinds, the late afternoon sun lighting up his eyes.

"That's not a social life," I said.

"GingerBoyUK and CrazyDogDude89 would disagree with you," he said with a wry smile. "They're my online gaming buddies."

"Yeah, I figured that," I said, doing my best to sound like a smartass.

"And what about your sex life, then?"

"I have a sex life, thank you very much, and his name is Jack," he said, quirking an eyebrow in my direction.

"Who's Jack?" I asked dubiously.

"Well, actually, that's not his full name. His full name is Fleshjack."

"Huh?"

Parker's pupils dilated as if he were a scientist who had just made a breakthrough discovery. A very naughty discovery.

"Wait. You don't know what a Fleshjack is?" he asked, not even bothering to try and conceal his smile.

I shook my head. "Nope, no idea."

"Oh, this is going to be good," Parker said as he walked over to the door.

"What are you doing?" I asked as he opened it.

"You'll see." He shot me a wicked look. "Hey, Dylan," he yelled as he stuck his head down the hallway. "Can you come here a sec, please?"

What was he doing? Dylan, our showrunner, showed up a few moments later and stood in the doorway. He was a nice guy, kinda average looking. He was in his thirties, but still dressed like he was in college.

My jaw dropped to the floor when Parker turned to look at me as he said, "Hey, Dylan, do you know what a Fleshjack is?"

I looked at the poor guy and blushed. But then Dylan saw my jaw on the floor, and decided to play some soccer with it.

"Oh yeah, a Fleshjack is a masturbator. I got a really good one from my girlfriend for my birthday. She paid extra and got the ultra-realistic one. It vibrates and everything."

"Thank you, Dylan," Parker said, his shit-eating grin fixed to his face.

"See, Dylan knows what it is," he said with both eyebrows arched.

"I'm—I'm in shock," I said.

I was.

I was a virgin when it came to sex, but was I also a virgin when it came to jacking off? Clearly, I was.

But if I thought Parker was finished, I was mistaken.

He stuck his head out the corridor again. "Hey, Jake, you got a minute?"

My eyes bulged in horror.

"No, not Jake," I pleaded.

Jake was our production manager and an all-around good guy in that old-fashioned, grandpa kind of way.

"He's always Santa at the Christmas party and his wife is Mrs. Claus," I added, but to no avail.

"What's up, Parker?" Jake asked as he stepped into my dressing room. "Oh, hey, Liam."

Clearly I hadn't managed to slink down and hide myself under the coffee table.

"Hey, Jake," I said sheepishly.

"Jake," Parker's voice rose in the air. "Would you happen to know what a Fleshjack is?"

"Oh sure," he replied instantly with a smile. A smile. Why was the man smiling? Why wasn't he trying to bury himself under the coffee table right beside me? "Elaine and I have tried to use one before, you know, to try and help with the premature ejaculation..."

Oh dear lord!

"But, yeah, not for me. I need the real thing, even if it only is for a few seconds."

"Thanks, Jake," Parker said, giving the man a pat on the shoulder. "That was very...insightful."

I waited until I heard the door shut before I rage-glared at Parker.

"You have ruined every single future Christmas party for me from now on," I half yelled at him, still cringing.

"In my defense," Parker said, "I had no idea he was going to go *there.*"

I covered my eyes. "All I can see is Mrs. Claus trying to help Santa with his premature ejaculation problem...and it's hurting my retinas."

"Oh, grow up," Parker said. I felt a soft pillow land against my side. "I made my point though, right? Everyone knows what a Fleshjack is, so there."

I wasn't going to look up at the tongue I was sure he was sticking out at me. I didn't want to give him the satisfaction.

"And my other point for the day is this—keep this thing with Hudson going. It is a goldmine, and your fast track to that promotion."

Something weird happened when Parker mentioned the promotion.

Normally it got me all excited on the inside, like I was internally rubbing my hands together with glee. It was what I had always wanted, what I had worked so hard for all of these years.

But this time when he said it, there was none of that giddy excitement. I didn't know what feeling had taken its place, but it felt heavier and darker. Like there was something inside of me that was resisting it.

That didn't make any sense at all. This was what I had always wanted. So why was it starting to feel...different?

"Hudson." Parker's voice snapped me out of my thoughts.

"Huh?" I looked over at him.

"When are you seeing Hudson next?" Parker said, and it sounded like he had been talking for a while. "Geez, what planet are you living on these days, Liam?"

I sat up a little straighter. "I'm seeing him tomorrow night. Remember, you said it would be good to be seen out in public?"

"Those do sound like my genius words, yes," Parker said, smiling. "Good, that's good. Go out. Be seen together. Be seen happy and smiling and...*kissing*."

My heart responded to that by skipping over itself a little. I guess that was normal, it was all part of the act. I mean, if I didn't have any feelings for my fake boyfriend, I wouldn't be able to pull this off. I was a meteorologist, not an actor.

Some feelings were okay and normal.

"Remember, Liam," Parker said, scrunching up his nose at me. "You're Daylesford's hottest piece of ass, and he's Daylesford's hottest alpha powertop. This is a match made in PR heaven."

CHAPTER TWELVE

LIAM

Heaven sure took a long time to roll around, but when it finally did, it definitely proved to be worth the wait. If heaven was a local weatherman's third fake date with an awesome, smart, charismatic, funny, caring guy, that is.

"How do you get used to this?" Hudson asked. He was perched across from me, sitting at a high table at No Name Bar. It was Daylesford's hippest new place to be seen, too hip to even have a name, except for calling itself No Name Bar.

"Get used to what?" I asked, looking up at the man through my lashes as I sipped my lemongrass-infused dry martini.

"It feels like everyone's watching us," he said, moving in a little closer. His forearm brushed lightly against mine and it sent a shiver through me.

"They're probably looking at you," I said. "You look absolutely amazing tonight."

He did, and the blush that was reddening his cheeks only

increased his attractiveness. Again, the man took a simple outfit—a black polo shirt and dark jeans—and turned it into an out-of-this-world viewing experience.

"No, no," he said with a deep laugh. "You are definitely the star of this relationship."

This *fake* relationship, I reminded myself, since for some reason, it had slipped his mind to add that word in.

I guess I had been in the public eye for so long that I had simply gotten used to the looks that were thrown my way, or having people whisper when I walked past, or people coming up to me asking for a selfie...or to say that stupid catchphrase.

So far this evening, things had been pretty chill. I only had one person come up for a selfie, and there were just a couple of photographers on the street, who accidentally on purpose caught us coming into the bar together. That was, as usual, Parker's handiwork.

"Does it bother you?" I asked Hudson. He'd agreed to be my fake boyfriend, he hadn't agreed to being made to feel like a public spectacle. "If this is in any way awkward or uncomfortable for you, just say the word and we'll leave."

I studied his face for any sign of a reaction.

He looked around the bar, scanning it with his light green eyes. Then he returned his gaze to me and shot me a warm smile.

"I'm good," he said in that rich voice of his. "But thank you for checking in."

I felt my skin prickling with heat, but I didn't know why, exactly.

A deep silence opened up between us.

I had been super busy with work, and Hudson was just as busy at his gym. Apparently our fake relationship was good for his business. I was glad that he was getting something out of it too. I didn't want everything to be all about me. Well, at least not all the time.

But between our hectic work schedules, we had only managed

to text over the last week. He would always be the one to initiate. A quick *hello, how was your day* type of text. Always at five past eight, when he knew I had finished my last broadcast for the evening. It was nice, but a little surprising at how quickly it had become so familiar.

"So tell me about these," I said, lazily grazing my fingertips over the brightly colored ink of his left bicep. "They're so beautiful and intricate."

I never really looked at them super closely before, but since I was talking about them, I figured it wouldn't be rude to stare.

"Oh, I see," Hudson said with a mock huff. "You only like me for my tattoos and my muscles, don't ya?"

"And your shaved head," I said, not peeling my eyes off his arms, his *massive, rock-solid* arms. "Don't forget about that."

I could feel his eyes on me and I knew he could see I was smiling.

"Are you being a naughty b—"

My fingers froze on a patch of dark green right above his elbow and I looked up to meet his gaze.

Boy?

Was he going to say boy?

"Tell me about your tattoos."

I'd been replaying our last conversation over and over in my head a million times during the past week.

The part where he had said he was a Daddy.

A Daddy who liked to teach and guide more than control and dominate.

A Daddy who thought sex was more than just a physical thing.

A Daddy who was...unconventional.

How was it that, for every one thing he told me about himself, I had ten questions spring up in my mind like a field of mushrooms?

"I was a really dumb kid, who got his first tattoo way too young," he said with a chuckle that made his whole torso bounce.

"How did you get a tattoo if you weren't old enough to?" I asked, continuing to study his arm.

"Fake ID," he said nonchalantly. "I was fifteen and this was my first ever tattoo."

He gently wrapped his hand around my fingers and guided them up the hard ridge of his well-defined tricep muscle.

"This?" I asked puzzled. It was a yellowy-orange vine, surrounded by intricate, deep green and blue vines that crept up his arm, disappearing under his shirt.

"Guess what it used to be?" he said smiling, as if he knew I would never be able to guess.

"What do you mean used to be?" I asked.

He chuckled again. "Everything that you see here and on my other arm has been done over. Like I said, I made some stupid choices, until I was about your age, actually. So, come on, guess, what was this first tattoo?"

His thick finger tapped on the orangey-yellow spot again.

"Don't know, maybe a sun?" I guessed.

He shook his head.

"I'm never going to get it, am I?"

"Nope," he said, reaching for his drink.

Damm, what else was yellow or orange and would be completely embarrassing to have as your first tattoo at the age of fifteen? My mind was drawing a complete and utter blank. I looked around the bar, as if some modern, minimalistic, too-cool-to-even-have-a-name hipster bar would provide the answer somehow.

I was just about to give up when I said the most random thing that popped into my head.

"I don't know...Tweety Bird," I said, expecting to be met with another chuckle.

Instead, I was met with silence.

"Yeah, that's right," Hudson said. The man was stunned, staring at me as if I had somehow broken into his childhood memory vault and rummaged around without permission.

"Are you serious?" I asked, bemused.

"Yeah, I can't believe you guessed that." He was still in shock.

"What can I say? I'm pretty good." I raised my glass in the air, and he matched it with his, giving it a hearty clink.

"That you are, my friend," he said.

His surprised face gave way to his impressed face. Although I was a lot less impressed with his word selection.

Friend?

Hmm...

"So, where do they go?" I asked, after taking a sip of my drink.

"The tattoos? They both run over my shoulder and then they come down over my pecs like this..."

He was tracing over his pecs with his index finger in a sort of round shape. It looked like the tattoos would cover most of his chest, stopping just above his nipples and leaving some space between them at the front of his chest.

"Television has ruined my imagination," I said flatly. "I might need you to show me sometime."

Take *that,* stupid friend comment.

Hudson's lips did this funny thing where they looked like they weren't sure what they were meant to be doing. They didn't want to smile, they definitely didn't want to pout, so what did that leave them with then? His eyes looked just as befuddled.

Luckily for him, we were interrupted by what looked like two college-aged guys, wanting a selfie.

After I obliged them, we had a few more drinks and continued with a lighthearted conversation.

"Whoa," Hudson said, looking at his phone. "It's almost midnight."

"Wait, was that a good whoa or a bad whoa?" I teased.

I wasn't much of a drinker, so the four drinks I'd drunk had left me feeling buzzy and a little...flirty.

"It was the good kind," he said, smiling in a way that reached all the way up to his eyes. "It was the *I can't believe how time flies when I'm having fun with you* kind of whoa."

He grabbed my hand.

Maybe he was feeling a little buzzy too?

Before I could brush off the thick layer of dust covering my flirting playbook, Hudson slapped the side of his head. "Oh shit, we haven't taken any photos tonight."

The man could go from alpha powertop to dreamboat cutie in under five seconds.

"Oh yeah," I said as I picked up my phone and I walked over to his side, leaning onto his broad shoulder. We'd been having such a good time that it had completely slipped my mind to document it for public consumption.

I quickly took some snaps. We both tilted and adjusted our heads every few seconds, like the selfie pros we were quickly becoming.

"There, that should do the trick," I said, closing down the camera on my phone.

I didn't move. I stayed there, my hands on his shoulders, his neck inches away from my mouth.

I felt a strong arm wrap around my waist as he pulled me into him. Before our lips could touch, I ducked down and gently nibbled on his neck. His mouth opened and a soft rumble escaped. It was the sexiest sound I had ever heard.

I ran my hand across his broad, hard chest and closed my eyes, imagining what his tattoos looked like under his shirt.

Slowly, I licked my way up his neck, across his slightly stubbled jawline, and over his chin, until I made it to his lower lip. His fingers dragged through my hair and pulled me up, his hungry tongue darting into my mouth. He was getting me into the perfect kissing position, and I let myself melt into it, moaning into his strength and power.

After nowhere near long enough, I pulled away.

"I need to use the bathroom," I said. I had been drinking, after all. "I'll be right back."

"Okay." His voice was reduced to barely more than a grunt.

"Stay right here," I said, smiling.

It was only as I made my way across the bar to the bathroom that I realized I had a massive hard-on. I clasped my hands in front of me, looked around, and prayed that no one would stop me for a selfie.

I managed to make it to the bathroom without any embarrassing fan incidents. But my relief was short-lived. The moment I entered the dimly lit, and surprisingly fresh-smelling bathroom, I heard two loud voices talking.

About me.

There were two men standing at the urinal, and clearly, they hadn't heard me come in.

"See that weather dude is here tonight with his new boyfriend?" the guy on the left said.

"Yeah," the man on the right snickered. "I bet that giant dude nails that little bitch bottom good."

I couldn't believe what I was hearing. I fell back against the wall and started to inch my way silently back toward the door.

"With an ass like that, can you blame him?" the guy on the left said.

"Ha, I can imagine him squealing like the little slut pig that he is."

I finally found the door and managed to get out and leave the sounds of oinking and laughing behind me.

My heart was racing like a freight train, and all I wanted was to get the hell out of there as fast as possible.

There was a reason Parker kept me off social media before he'd had a chance to clean up the comments. He'd always said people could be cruel, but hearing it like that made me feel so...worthless.

Was that really how people saw me? As some slutty sex pig?

All of a sudden, everything got a whole lot realer. Sure, Parker and I played into my sexuality, but it was always in a fun and friendly way. In a Mrs. Langley-approved way.

Not in some gross, *drunk men pissing at a urinal and talking about me like I was a piece of garbage* kind of way.

I ran over to where Hudson was sitting. I could feel my face was flushed as I reached him.

"What's wrong?" His concern was immediate and palpable.

"Can we get outta here?" I said, grabbing my jacket off the back of the chair. "Now, please?"

"Of course," he said, helping me with my jacket, which had gotten caught on the chair. He then quickly grabbed his own jacket, and interlaced his fingers with my sweaty, cold ones. He led me out of there without delay and without asking a single question.

At least, not until we stepped outside. The cool air felt good against my hot face.

"Can we go back to your place? Please?" I asked, doing everything I could to hold it together.

"Sure," he said with a firm nod. "Let's go."

CHAPTER THIRTEEN

HUDSON

My heart stayed firmly lodged in my throat when I saw Liam returning visibly upset from the bathroom, and it stayed there right until I took him back to my place, sat him down on my couch, and made him a hot cup of tea.

In between, there was a completely silent car ride. I kept looking over at him while he stared blankly out the window.

He wasn't crying and he wasn't in any obvious pain or distress. I did ask him before we got in my car, and he said that he was physically fine, but I still had no freaking idea what had gotten him so riled up.

Up until that point, the evening had been going so well.

Liam was so great to talk to, and I found it easy to open up to him. There was something about him that made me feel like he was seeing me differently than most other guys saw me. As if, somehow, he wasn't applying the same filter and the same preconceptions that other people did.

When he asked me about my tattoos, he wanted to find out the story behind them. He wasn't simply lusting after them like so many men did. He seemed to be genuinely interested in getting to know me better.

But now all I cared about was knowing what had happened to make him this upset.

He blew across the top of the cup, creating little ripples in the tea. I sat down, far enough away from him to give him his own space, but close enough to be able to reach out and touch his hand...eventually.

When he was ready.

Whatever had happened was obviously painful. I needed to proceed with caution. I was going to take this slowly.

"You have a nice place here," Liam said as he took his first sip of tea, glancing around the room. We were sitting in my study, my favorite room in the house. It was cozy. I loved to have the fire going on a cold winter's night, grab the blanket my grandma had given me when I was a boy, and get lost in a good book or movie.

"Thanks," I replied.

"You been here long?" he asked in a low voice.

"Let's see, coming up on ten years actually," I said after thinking about it for a moment, surprising myself at how long it had been.

I loved my house and I had been super proud of myself buying it after I turned thirty. The gyms were going great at that point, but it was still a massive investment for me.

Thankfully, I was smart with my money and managed to pay it off by the time I hit forty, which was a good thing given the state of my business at the moment. At least I owned my house outright.

Liam seemed satisfied with my answer and continued to drink the tea in silence. After a few minutes, and once I could sense that his energy had calmed, I decided to speak.

"Liam," I said, and without delay, his eyes met mine.

He was fully alert, but there was a raw vulnerability just under the surface of his skin, like exposed electrical cables.

"I'm going to ask you a few questions. You don't have to answer anything you don't want to. I want you to know that's okay. There's no pressure or obligation. Do you understand?"

"Yes," he said, looking deep into his mug.

"Good." I got a little more comfortable on the couch before saying, "I'd like to check in with you and see how you're feeling now."

He took another sip, letting the hot drink swirl around in his mouth for a while. "I feel ashamed and like I'm the world's biggest fool."

That was not the answer I had been expecting. What the hell had happened back there? I had no idea, all I knew was that I needed to tread carefully.

"Is how you're feeling now because of something that happened back at the bar?" I asked, pretty much knowing what the answer would be, but wanting to double-check just in case.

"Yes."

The sadness in his voice tugged at my heart and made me want to reach out and comfort him with my touch. But it was too soon for that. We had to talk about it, whatever it was, first.

"Do you feel comfortable telling me what happened back there?" I asked as gently as I could.

He nodded, but stayed quiet for a while. I could see the struggle going on behind his gray eyes. It felt like he was warring with himself, and possibly still deciding how much he really wanted to tell me.

After all, I was only his fake boyfriend.

"I know I'm a bit of a joke," he said with a quiver.

"What? No, Liam. You're not a joke. Why would you think that?"

Again, I was totally surprised at the direction he was going in.

"It's okay, Hudson," he said, and for the first time since we had left the bar, a slight smile fell on his face. "I *am* a bit of a joke, but I'm also *in* on the joke. You know?"

I didn't quite know where he was going with this, but I didn't say anything. I just gave a warm smile to encourage him to keep talking.

"That was one of the reasons why I brought Parker, my publicist, on about two years ago. Hard work only gets you so far in this industry. If you want to get ahead, you have to really stand out."

"You're very good at standing out," I said.

We both giggled.

"Yes, I am," he said. "Parker has been very good at getting me attention. Wearing colorful bow ties, Waistcoat Wednesdays, Rate My Shirt Saturday, wearing tight pants that show off my ridiculously large ass..."

"Your award-winning large ass," I said, and he laughed so sweetly it made me want to lean closer and touch him more than ever. Laughing suited him and he remained light, even though his next words were a little heavier.

"But see, that's what I mean. It's all a bit of a joke, really. I'm not saying it in a bad way, I just mean that I've had to do things to get attention in order to hopefully get ahead in my career."

I pushed the thought of his promotion aside, not wanting to be consumed by that right now.

"Even us," he continued.

"Us?"

"Yeah, this whole fake relationship thing that we're doing. It's kind of silly when you think about it."

"So, what does all of this have to do with what happened tonight?" I asked, finding myself strangely ruffled by him calling what we were doing *silly*.

In an instant, his lightness disappeared.

"When I went to the bathroom, I overheard two guys talking about me. Well, about us, actually." His chest was heaving, so I pointed at his tea, a gentle reminder for him to take his time and stay as calm as he could.

"What did they say?" I finally prodded.

"They called me all sorts of things. Awful things, Hudson." I saw his bottom lip begin to quiver and tears welling in his eyes.

"You can stop if you want to, but I would like to know," I said, sliding a little closer to him. For support, if he needed it.

Tears threatened to spill out of his eyes as he turned to me and said, "They were making fun of my ass and calling me a *little bottom bitch*. They said I was a *slut pig*."

The last few words were barely audible, but the hurt was unmissable.

Before the first tear fell down his cheek, I took his mug of tea out of his hands and placed it on the table, before wrapping my arms around him, wishing desperately my arms could shield him from the pain he was feeling.

"It's okay, it's okay," I whispered as I rocked him back and forth.

I could feel his entire body sobbing, but he needed to get it out. What an awful thing to have to experience. His tears soaked through my shirt and felt warm against my flesh.

Once he had gotten it all out, he pulled away and began to brush the tears away.

"Oh my goodness," he said. "I am so sorry about that. I'm so embarrassed."

He kept drying his eyes, but his movements were harsh and rough.

"Hey," I said, grabbing his hands to still him. "You have nothing to be embarrassed about, Liam. And you have no reason to feel ashamed for anything. You are not a fool, or any of the things those guys said. They were idiots. They have to talk shit about someone else to make themselves feel better. What does that tell you about their own self-esteem?"

Liam looked at me, and his swollen red eyes softened.

"You sound like a psychologist already," he teased softly.

I smiled. I didn't know what to say. I wasn't trying to be a psychologist. I was just trying to be a real friend to my fake boyfriend.

Now *that* was something worth analyzing.

"Do you want to know what the real funny thing is?" Liam asked as he wiped away the last of his tears.

"Sure," I replied, shuffling back to give him a little more room.

He took a deep breath, turned to face me square-on and said, "Even though I have this ass, this award-winning ass..."

He smiled and took another deep breath.

"I'm actually a virgin."

"Oh."

I was starting to lose track of how many times Liam had surprised me that evening. I wasn't expecting *that*. Not because of his ass, obviously, but because he was twenty-seven, good-looking, and successful, so I'd just assumed he'd slept with guys before.

"So not only were those guys idiots," Liam said, "they were also completely wrong about me."

I knew that feeling very well myself.

"I guess they were," I said. "Can I ask why you've never had..."

"Sex?" he jumped in.

I nodded. "Yeah."

"I guess I just never had the time for a boyfriend..."

"Even at university?" I pressed.

I understood that he was dedicated to his career and that it basically took over his entire life, but he hadn't always been working. There was a time in his life when he was simply a student...and students liked to fuck. A lot.

"I mean, yeah," he said with an uneasy shrug.

"Can I say something, Liam?" I asked.

"Sure."

I ran my tongue behind my teeth while I considered my next words.

"In the time we've spent together, I've noticed that you have two voices. Your professional weatherman voice and your real voice. So, you don't have to tell me anything more, and I won't press you any further, but the answer you just gave was in your professional voice."

Liam stared down at the floor for a moment.

I worried I had pushed too hard. He had already experienced one form of shame tonight, the last thing I wanted to do was to add to it.

Just as I was about to apologize, he looked up and spoke.

"You're right," he said. "That was a bullshit answer."

He sighed loudly.

"I suppose I've just never really been that interested in sex for some reason. Or guys in general, for that matter. So it was always just easier to throw myself into my studies or my career and use that as an excuse."

"It's okay not to be interested in sex," I said. "Some people aren't. I hate using labels, but have you considered that you may be asexual?"

"No." He said it with such force that it caught me by surprise. "I mean, yes I have considered it, but I don't think it's the right fit for me."

"Why not?" I asked, hoping I was coming across as supportive and not nosy.

"Because recently, I've been having feelings."

"What sort of feelings?" I asked with a gentle heat rising from my chest.

"Sexual feelings."

"Oh...what sort of sexual feelings?"

"About you."

I swallowed. "Right."

"Is that okay?" he asked, biting down on his lower lip.

"It is," I replied.

We then fell into a silence which should have been awkward, but it wasn't.

I think we both just needed some time to process the events of that evening, because a lot had happened, and in a way it was nice that we were able to do that in quietness, together.

"What are you thinking?" he asked after a good chunk of time had gone by, narrowing his eyes at me.

I took some time to think about it before answering. "I admire your ability to process your feelings and be able to be vulnerable. That's a hard thing to do, and not a lot of people can do it."

"Right, Dr. Madden, very good answer," he said with a cheeky smirk.

He'd caught me.

I had defaulted to a quasi-professional-slash-distant mode.

This time, I was the one putting on a professional voice and avoiding talking personally.

Why?

What was I avoiding?

CHAPTER FOURTEEN

HUDSON

The sound of leaves crackling underfoot filled the thick, moss-laden air around me. It was an unusually dreary day with a gray, cloud-filled sky and occasional bursts of a chilly wind that served to unsettle me even more.

Ever since Liam had come back to my place after our date at the bar, I had been left with a feeling like I was being submerged under water. I was heavy, yet weightless. I was cold, yet refreshed.

It left me feeling disorientated at first, like I had woken up in a strange house with no memory of how I had gotten there. But slowly, the fog lifted, and it gave way to the most beautiful path forward. It was the crystal clear wake-up call I didn't even know I needed.

Funny how a fake relationship could be the catalyst to awaken some very real feelings.

I went into this whole thing a little blindsided and a lot green. Really, I just wanted to spend a little more time with my crush.

When we began, I wasn't ready for anything more. But now I was beginning to realize that I wasn't ready to settle for anything less.

For the last four years, ever since Richie had died, I had been keeping distance between myself and any guy who showed the faintest sign of interest in me.

For the first three years, having space had served me well. I needed to deal with what happened with Richie, and I'm not ashamed to say that I gave my heart all the time it needed to heal and to recover.

After all, the heart is a muscle. Whenever I trained hard at the gym and really gave a workout my all, I would take at least a day, sometimes two, to recover. Most people didn't realize that that's where all the good stuff happens, in the recovery. Muscles break down, then they build back up again. And when they rebuild, they're stronger than ever before.

But after three years, I realized I had become stuck in recovery mode. I knew I wasn't ready for anything serious or long-term, but I had shut myself off from even the possibility of a date, dinner, going to the movies, or watching *Romy and Michele's High School Reunion* at my place.

That was why I agreed to be Liam's fake boyfriend. It was a way for me to dip my toes back into the pool without the risk of things getting serious or of anyone getting hurt.

We had moved past that point now.

Or, at least, I had.

For Liam, our fake relationship was simply a means to an end. I understood that when we started things, and I knew that his eyes were firmly fixed on the prize. A promotion to national. It had nothing to do with being with me.

I guess I had my eyes on something too. A different kind of prize. I needed to let go, to forgive, and to finally say a proper goodbye.

Today was a day for endings.

I continued making my way up the central path, looking out at the dull headstones all around me. As far as cemeteries went, Brookhaven was a nice one. It was located on the outskirts of Daylesford by a lake, so it was a peaceful, tranquil setting to deal with whatever emotions came up, surrounded by the beauty of nature. The scenery provided some much-needed reassurance and hope.

I brushed my hand along the trunk of the beautiful red maple, the way I had every month for the last four years when I had come to pay my respects to Richie.

This time, it felt different.

My senses were buzzing, acutely attuned to every single detail around me. The chill in the air, the smell of wet leaves, the coarseness of the red maple bark as I grazed it with my fingertips.

Eventually, I veered to the right, following the familiar, well-worn path I had taken so many times, until I finally reached his headstone.

I placed the flowers I had bought from the old lady by the side of the road onto the ground beside the headstone, arranging them as neatly as I could. I smiled. He always liked things neat and tidy. I did too, or at least, I thought I did until I met him. Richie was next-level.

Normally, I would sit down for a few minutes and just let whatever I was feeling wash through me. But today, the restlessness inside of me made me feel like standing for a little longer.

I looked up at the forlorn sky. As I did, the sun broke through the clouds and a ray of sunshine beamed down onto me. I exhaled, enjoying the warmth of the sun hitting my face.

I still felt a little unsettled, so I paced around a little bit, unsure of what I was feeling.

Guilt was definitely coming up for me. As it always did. An all-too-easy-to-recall reel of memories flooded back too. All the things I could have said differently.

Maybe if I hadn't broken up with him two weeks earlier, he never would have...

I shook my head, breaking free from that rabbit hole as the clouds overtook the sun again. A cold shiver ran through me.

I was also feeling sadness and a sense of irreversible loss. No matter what I thought or felt now, it wouldn't make the tiniest shred of difference. Nothing could ever change what had happened.

And then there were the slightest slivers of anger, but nowhere near what I used to feel.

All of the usual emotions, really, but strangely, they were all in check. I felt in control. Maybe having gone through them as often as I had, had in some ways diminished their hold over me.

For years, it felt like I was trapped in a blazing inferno, unable to get out, suffocating in the flames. Now it felt like I was looking at a small fire, nothing serious. It was a fire that was happening in the distance, away from me.

I took it as a sign that I was about to do the right thing.

I was ready.

This was going to be the last time I visited Richie every month. I still wanted to visit him yearly, but on his birthday, not on the anniversary of his death. I wanted to remember and honor his life, because he was so much more to me than just the way he'd died.

The whirl of emotions I was feeling in my chest started to release, and I sat down. The sun broke through again, shining down brightly. I raised my head toward it, basking in the warmth. I exhaled loudly and decided to lie down on the ground, facing the ever-changing sky.

The wind had picked up a bit, so I zipped my jacket up nice and tight. I stared at the clouds in the sky as they drifted past. Most of them were a deep, dark gray color, and with the wind, they were breaking apart and then reconnecting quickly.

My mind went to Liam.

I pictured him as a child, lying on the ground, looking up at the clouds with his twin brother, the way I was now. I guessed his work made him think of his brother, and in some way, kept Toby alive for him. It was good to keep the people we had loved and lost close to us.

I remembered him telling me about how he and his brother would look at the shapes of the clouds, trying to identify them. Or how, after his brother died, the clouds spoke to him in a way, conveying feelings rather than objects.

I looked around the expansive sky and tried to find shapes or meaning in the clouds. One did look like a lopsided truck, but even that was a bit of a stretch. And meaning? They were moving too fast and changing form too quickly for me to really decipher anything deeper.

Was I really looking for a sign in the sky?

I shook my head and let out a small laugh. That was something kids did. Here I was, a man in his forties, doing the same.

And yet, I couldn't help but be disappointed that I didn't get a clear signal from the clouds. Something that was as bright and clear as day, and that would let me know that I was on the right path...or not.

But the clouds just kept moving at an almost relentless pace, breaking apart and then reforming before drifting off and out of sight.

I sat up and stared silently at the headstone. I never talked to it. That felt weird to me, and it had freaked me out the one time that I did do it. Richie was dead, and wherever he was, he could hear my thoughts. That felt right to me.

So I sat, and I stared, and I let my thoughts run through me freely. I thought of all the good times we had together, because we did have a lot of them. Richie loved Florida, so we went once, sometimes twice a year. We'd stay in the same room at the same resort and...he just loved it.

He was terrible in the kitchen, but he was always in there, fussing over something. Always cleaning, or tidying, or doing...something. He liked being active and couldn't stay still for long.

When my mind wanted to return to an argument we'd had, or some still-unresolved issue that sat hidden away in the darkest recesses of my mind, I knew it was time to think it.

Goodbye, Richie.

Today was a day for endings.

I stood up, and took one final look at the headstone before making my way back, past the red maple and down the path to my car. As I walked, I felt the light wetness of tears that I hadn't realized had fallen on my face. They were tears of forgiveness and release.

I forgave Richie for what happened.

I forgave myself for what happened too, and I released myself from all the burden I had been carrying. Once and for all.

"Hudson?" Liam's voice ripped me out of my thoughts.

He was sitting by a headstone.

"Liam," I said, hurriedly wiping away the tears from my face. "What—what are you doing here?"

I only realized how stupid a question that was to ask someone at a cemetery after I had asked it.

"I'm here for Toby. It's the anniversary of his death today."

"I'm sorry," I said as I approached him.

Liam stood up and gave me a hug. I wanted to draw him in closer, but he pulled away before I could.

"My folks will be here soon. We do this every year. Mom packs a picnic basket full of his favorite food, and then we go sit by the lake and eat it together."

"That sounds really nice," I said.

"What are you doing here?" he asked as a puzzled look swept over his face. Shit, I hadn't told him about Richie...or at least, about how he had died.

"Visiting..."

"A friend? A relative?" Liam asked, and there was an undercurrent of anxiety in his tone that I couldn't quite figure out.

"A boyfriend, actually," I said. "A former boyfriend. Richie."

"I see."

I couldn't read the expression on his face. This was already a sad day for him, and I'd probably just added an unnecessary element of surprise to it.

"Do you want to come over to my place later tonight, once you're all done with your family?" I asked, and a spark of hope flickered momentarily in his eyes.

I bit down on my tongue and pretended I didn't see it.

"Sure," he said. "Say, seven?"

"That sounds good. I'll see you then, Liam."

With another light hug, I was off. My mind was already a million miles in front of me, thinking ahead to the evening.

I knew I had to tell him. This fake relationship thing that we were doing just couldn't continue anymore. I couldn't keep going like this.

Today was a day for endings.

CHAPTER FIFTEEN

LIAM

My spidey senses were telling me that something was wrong. Even though the twenty-first was always a tough day for me because of Toby, I could still sense it.

From the moment I had seen Hudson at the cemetery earlier that day, I'd felt it. His embrace wasn't as strong or as close as it usually was. The man was basically the poster child for bear hugs, and the two hugs he had given me that day were cub hugs at best.

Then there was the look on his face when he said why he was there, who he was visiting. A boyfriend. Clearly someone he still loved and was attached to. He had never spoken about him before, but I guess I hadn't really asked either. Still, I couldn't help but feel a little...I didn't know what, really. I knew I had no right to feel jealous, but it wasn't quite jealousy. It was more a feeling of being...left out, somehow. Again, something I had no right to be feeling.

Then there was the way he was being with me, ever since I'd

arrived at his place half an hour earlier. Greeted by a weak cub hug *again*, I knew he was being evasive. He kept avoiding direct eye contact with me as much as he could. He wasn't saying a lot himself, and he didn't seem particularly interested in what I was saying either.

He had just finished making a hearty chicken salad, and we sat down at the table just off his kitchen.

"This is good, thank you," I said after taking a bite. "Better than hot dogs, cookies, and chocolate mud cupcakes. I guess it's no surprise that eight-year-olds don't exactly have a refined palate."

"True," Hudson said, and for the first time that evening, smiled warmly.

The thumping in my chest eased a little. Maybe I was just being overly sensitive? Maybe everything was fine and I was just imagining things?

But no, my spidey sense was never wrong.

"Are you okay?" Hudson asked between mouthfuls. "I know today must have been a hard day for you, but you seem a little extra tense."

"I'm fine," I lied, shoveling in a forkful of salad into my mouth to avoid having to say anything else.

It seemed to do the trick, and we moved on to some more lighthearted conversation.

"Let's go into the living room," Hudson said once we had finished our meal. He got up and took my plate.

"Thank you, that was delicious," I said. "My body needed something clean."

He smiled warmly and my shoulders loosened.

He took the dishes to the sink. His kitchen was a pretty decent size, but his massive frame hulking over the sink made it look small. I could see his shoulders rising and falling with every breath he took.

He then turned around, and said the words that no one in a

relationship—even if it was a fake relationship—ever wanted to hear. "We need to talk."

He led the way from the kitchen to his nicely appointed living room. It was modern but had a homely feel to it. There were masculine hues of brown and gray splashed throughout. I noticed a few shelves proudly displaying a collection of silver trophies, which I assumed were from his weightlifting days, on the bookcase and there was a massive eighty inch TV screen against the far wall.

As I glanced around the room, I couldn't help but wonder if his previous partner, Richie, had lived with him. Was this their house? Or did they each have their own place?

I looked around for signs of anything that wasn't Hudson's, but couldn't find anything. Suddenly, a heavy pit formed in my stomach. It was guilt for being so self-absorbed that I didn't know any of this stuff about Hudson.

"So," Hudson said, once we had both sat down on his plush and supremely comfortable brown leather sofa. "I want to talk to you about us. Fake us, I mean."

Dread, sorrow, and guilt rose up into a lump in my throat. But more than anything else, I felt annoyed.

He was going to end things between us, and I was annoyed that I hadn't done more to get to know him. Because what I knew of the man so far, I liked. Very much.

I debated trying to rush in and say something. But what could I say that would make him change his mind and not make me sound like a desperate, clingy fake boyfriend?

So I just slipped into that all-too-familiar professional mode, looked up at him with a forced smile, and said, "Sure, what would you like to talk about?"

He shot a funny look my way, but didn't call me out on my demeanor. There was no point in delaying the inevitable, I guessed. He probably just wanted to get it over and done with as quickly as possible and return to his normal life. A life without me and all of my crazy, idiotic, publicity-seeking schemes.

"When we met with Parker to figure out how this," he motioned with his hand between us, "would work, we talked about a lot of things. But we never discussed an end date or an exit strategy."

I knew it.

Even though I was expecting it, it felt like a kick in the gut.

I knew we'd only known each other for a few weeks. It wasn't like we had been dating forever. And on top of all of that, it had been a fake relationship right from the get-go.

"No, we didn't," I said, looking down.

Hudson's fingers grazed my chin and he softly tilted my head back up. His light green eyes were filled with a cimmerian shade I had never seen before.

I slipped out of his fingers and looked away. I had to. I couldn't stare into his eyes as he said what I knew he was about to say. It would be too hard.

"Liam, I think we should end this arrangement we have," he said.

His voice was emotionless. I was staring at a spot on his rug, mooring myself to it, fighting against the torrent of emotions raging inside of me.

"I can't be fake boyfriends anymore," he added.

There was just the slightest inkling of sadness in the way he said it, that caught my breath and forced my eyes back onto him.

"Is it because of your boyfriend?" I asked. "The one you were visiting in the cemetery today?"

It had to be. Nothing else had changed between us.

"No." Hudson's answer surprised me, especially how strong and forceful it sounded.

"It's not?" I wasn't entirely convinced.

"It's not," he said, sounding even more adamant than before. "It's because of you."

"Me?" I was taken aback. "Have I done something wrong? Have I upset you or offended you in some way? If I have, I'm really—"

"Liam, stop," he said as a smile stretched across his lips. "You haven't done anything bad or wrong. Quite the opposite, in fact."

"I—I don't get it." I knew I'd had an emotional day, but the guy really wasn't making any sense.

"I've never told you this before, because I didn't want to freak you out and sound like some crazy fan, but I didn't just have a little crush on you. I had a massive crush on you...for about the last year and a half."

"Really?" I asked, my eyes wide with surprise.

"Yeah, you can ask my friends and they'll confirm. They've enjoyed ribbing me out about it way more than good friends should."

His words were serious, but his smile let me know that he was okay with it.

"We had even seen you out and about during that time," he continued, and I noticed for the first time that his face looked flushed. "Six times, actually. I saw you out at bars or around town six times, and I never approached you."

"Why not?" I asked, puzzled...and a little flattered.

He took a breath as he considered his next words. "I guess because I wasn't ready for anything more than just a crush. When Richie—that's who I was at the cemetery for today—died almost four years ago, it took me a long time to deal with it properly."

"I'm sure," I said, hoping to sound as empathetic as I was feeling.

"I loved Richie," he continued. "But it was a complicated and fiery relationship. Ultimately, I knew we weren't meant for each other."

He paused.

"There were too many ways that we just weren't compatible."

I nodded, but wasn't going to intrude by asking for more details. If he wanted to give them, he could. But if not, that was fine too.

"And then late one evening not too long ago, my TV crush walked into my real-life gym."

"Oh yeah?" I said, brightening up. "And how did that work out for you?"

"Brilliantly," he said, and my heart literally skipped a beat. "You gave me exactly what I needed. I was crushing on you and it felt safe. And this fake relationship arrangement of ours also gave me what I needed...for a while."

"But not anymore?" I asked nervously.

"No," he said, under his breath. "I like you, Liam. As in, I like you...for real..."

"I really like you too," I interrupted, but my words were met with a somber look.

"Which is why I think it would be the healthy, smart option to end this fake relationship. I'm..." His voice faltered, so he sat up taller as he cleared his throat. "I'm not ready to get hurt again."

"I'm not going to hurt you, Hudson," I said, and I'd never meant anything more in my life.

"I know you wouldn't do it *intentionally*," Hudson said, and I frowned at his intonation on the last word. "But this isn't what you really want, Liam. You want a promotion and to move to New York to be on *Wake Up America*. That's why we're doing this whole thing, isn't it?"

Was it?

It had certainly started off that way, but now I didn't know. Well, I did, but I wasn't sure if I was ready to face my feelings. All I knew was that Hudson made me come alive and made me feel things I had never felt before.

He awakened dormant desires and feelings of sexual attraction that I'd thought I was doomed to live my life without.

I always thought there was something wrong with me. That was why I put on a mask and showed the world a side of me that I thought they would love and accept. Hudson, simply by the way he talked to me, asked me questions, and really listened, showed me that he wanted to peel off that mask and get to know the guy underneath it.

That was...seriously scary.

I felt the pressure of his gaze on me.

"No, I...I mean we...this is...er, I don't know exactly."

It was a shitty answer, but it was the best that I could do.

"Why do we have to label this?" I asked after a few moments of racking my brain, trying to come up with something more intelligent. "You like me. I like you. We're having a good time together...why does it need to be neatly tied up? Why can't this—whatever this is between us—just...happen?"

"Hmpf."

It was one of the cutest sounds I had heard escaping the man's lips, and probably the closest thing he would ever get to a pout as well.

I was pleased I had made a good point, but more than that, I was excited he seemed to think it was a good point too. Excited in a way I had only ever felt with him. It was a deep, body-level excitement that I could feel from the top of my head to the bottom of my feet, but also around my groin, and my hardening cock.

No man had ever had this effect on me. I shuffled toward him, grabbed his shirt with both hands, and pulled him into me.

Our kiss was rough and wet and filthy. As my tongue wildly explored the inside of his mouth, I straddled him. I spread my knees out, farther and farther away from his body, bringing my ass lower and lower onto his bulging erection. I rubbed my ass against the length of him, and he let out a low growl that made me tremble.

I ran my hand across his face, along his smooth head, and down onto his broad shoulders. He was all smooth skin and hard muscle. His fingers were gently playing with my lower stomach under my shirt, grazing my light hairs with a giddy innocence that left me wanting...more.

With my pulse racing, I unzipped my jeans and pulled them, and my boxer briefs, down my legs. My hard cock sprang out and was instantly met by Hudson's warm, capable hands. He ran his fingers delicately along the entire length of it. I dropped my head back and spread my knees even wider, rubbing my ass on the hard cock that was throbbing in his jeans.

My heart was beating fast at the sheer audacity of what I was doing. Pants bunched up around my knees, straddling a man who was jacking me off. This was the wildest, craziest sex thing I had ever done. And I fucking loved it.

Years of repression and feeling bad about lacking desire, that spark that drove people to do crazy things like this, peeled right off me like paint off a wall. I broke through whatever it was that had been holding me back. My body was surging with a feeling of pure, unbridled freedom.

This was my sexual awakening.

But if I thought that Hudson would just give me a simple handjob, I was very, *very* mistaken.

I looked down and saw Hudson staring at my cock as if he were mesmerized by it. He reached his hand out, placing the flat part of this palm against my glistening cockhead. I did my best not to, but I shuddered involuntarily. He looked up at me with a questioning look.

"I'm sorry," I whispered, feeling the familiar tide of shame inflaming my body. "I precum a lot."

"Don't apologize," came Hudson's steady reply as he kept his eyes glued to mine. "You don't ever need to feel bad about your body, or how it reacts. Alright, Liam?"

"Uh...okay."

His words felt so good and yet so foreign at the same time. I had spent a lifetime criticizing every part of myself and my body, but it felt freeing to have permission to let it all just...disappear. My leaking cock was right up there, close to the top of my body-shame list.

He pressed his hand against my wet cockhead and started to rub around the crown of my cock in small, flat-palmed circles. The sensation was tender and sweet, yet left me desperate for more at the same time.

Once the precum started to dry up, he eased off. He squeezed the slit of my swollen head to release another drop of juicy precum, and then began rubbing his hand around my purple head. It sent tingles of pleasure roaring though my body and made me feel giddy.

Then, he stopped the movement but kept his palm firmly pressed against the tip of my dick. He stretched his fingers out like tentacles. It reminded me of a claw machine you'd see at a games arcade—an X-rated claw machine—as his fingertips gently slid along the length of my shaft. My body rocked in time with the delicate movement of his fingers, and I could feel the pressure building deep inside me.

The look of concentration on his face almost made me lose it. His eyes were lasered in on my cock, his tongue sticking out the corner of his mouth. It was like my cock was the only thing that existed in his world.

I'd never felt more wanted, more beautiful, or more free.

"What—what are you doing?" I somehow managed to get the words out.

He looked up at me with the most tantalizing smile stretching his lips. "You like it?"

Did he even need to ask?

I nodded like an idiot, barely managing to pant out a, "Yes, I like it a lot."

He returned his gaze to my cock and kept up the claw-like movement that felt like heaven.

"It's called crowning," he said calmly. "It's a gentle but intense tantric masturbation technique."

It sure fucking was.

As much as the pleasure he was creating in my body felt amazing, seeing him playing with my cock, hearing him talk about what he was doing to me, filled me with an even greater excitement. It felt so forbidden, but also like it was the most natural thing in the world too.

"What about you?" I said, noticing that Hudson was still fully dressed. He hadn't made the slightest motion toward his own cock, which I could see straining through his pants. I wanted to see him naked too, although a part of me was enjoying the dynamic as well, with him fully clothed and my cock out. I felt raw and vulnerable, but not exposed or uncomfortable.

He looked up at me again with a wicked gleam in his eyes. "This is all about you, baby. Let me please you."

I threw my head back as he wrapped his fingers around the base of my cock and with steady, firm strokes, fisted it all the way up to my swollen head, before bringing it all the way back down. I felt my balls tightening and the pressure in my cock approaching the point of no return.

"Come for me," he said as his strokes became more furious, his stare more intense. With just a few more strong, fast movements up and down the length of my dick, I finally exploded.

I unleashed my cum all over him, lost in the shuddering release that escaped my body. He squeezed the last drop out of me by gently pinching my slit. He raised his fingers to his mouth and tasted me.

But then...he didn't stop like I was expecting him to.

Instead, he kept stroking my cock, with such gentleness that I had to look down to see if he was even touching it at all.

"Keep breathing," he said as he looked up at me. "Nice, slow and steady breaths. You can do it, Liam."

I had no idea what he was doing, but with a quick nod I focused on my breathing like never before. In and out...in and out...my cock twitched in Hudson's hand. It was probably just as confused about what was happening as I was.

Normally by this point it would start to soften and become almost too painful to even touch. But because Hudson's hands were soft, so gentle, any little bit of discomfort I felt was overtaken by the calming effect he was having on me.

After a few minutes of tender stroking, my cock slowly began to spring back to life again. As it got harder, Hudson's pressure increased as well.

"Keep breathing," he reminded me as my breath caught in my chest.

I was dazed by what the man was doing to me.

When my cock became fully hard, Hudson placed the flat of his palm against my slit. It was so sensitive that I pulled away involuntarily. I couldn't even help it.

"Keep breathing, Liam. Slow and steady. You can do this."

He brought his palm back against my cockhead, and this time, I felt a jolt of pleasure, not pain.

"Good, there you go." I couldn't tell whether Hudson was talking to me or my cock. But I was starting to feel *really* good.

Despite having come just moments before, I felt my body chasing another orgasm. I didn't even know that it was possible to do that.

But as Hudson started clawing away at my cock like he had before, his fingertips gliding up and down the smooth surface of my dick, I felt the build-up surge within me again.

The momentum wasn't as strong or as big as the first time, but after a few moments, my body rocked as another wave of release flowed out of me.

"Oh my god, oh my god," I panted as Hudson squeezed out the last drops of cum from my completely spent cock.

"Come next to me," he said. "Lie down here and relax."

I brought my legs over one side of him and snuggled into his warm chest. Feelings of euphoria were still rushing through me, but they were slowly starting to settle.

"That was amazing," I breathed into his beefy pec. I looked up at him and could see the happiness written all over his face.

He stroked my hair and l let out a series of soft moans into his chest, my body still coming down from its multi-orgasmic high.

Finally, finally, my feet touched the ground and I landed back on planet earth.

"You see," I said with a goofy, post-double-orgasm smile as I leaned up to look at him. "We don't have to label anything. That wasn't even sex and it was the most amazing thing I've ever felt."

I snuggled even closer into the giant man. For a moment he stiffened and I felt like something was wrong, but then he wrapped me up in his arms again and pressed a delicate kiss on my forehead.

CHAPTER SIXTEEN

HUDSON

"Why are you being so good tonight?" Porter asked, returning from the bar with two drinks in hand.

"Thanks," I said, taking the lemonade from him. "I just didn't feel like drinking, that's all."

"Fine, fine," Porter said as he sat down at the window seat next to me. "You know me. I would never peer-pressure someone into doing anything."

His words were true, but whenever he tried to sound innocent when he spoke, it always made me chuckle. Porter was many things, but innocent was not one of them.

We were still in the midst of our *just turned forty and having an existential crisis* phase. Which, for us, meant that we still hadn't found a proper replacement bar for The Laird. Steel had only just started construction on his new bar last week, so we were still a good five or six months away from finding our new forever bar.

"Where are Steel and Stirling? They're gonna be joining us,

right?" I asked.

I really hoped so. I needed their advice, and as much as I loved Porter and knew I could talk to him about anything, I wanted to hear a couple of other opinions about this.

Right on cue, both of our phones vibrated.

"Here we go," Porter said, smacking his lips. "The excuse parade begins."

I lifted my phone and saw he was right. Two texts. From two excuse-laden Daddies.

"Stirling's out," I said, reading his message. "Mikey's mom isn't doing well. It's nothing too serious, but they just want to spend the night with her to make sure she's okay."

"That sucks about Mikey's mom," Porter said with a worried look. "Early onset dementia is terrible."

"It is," I agreed. "I'm just texting Stirling back to say *no worries* and to give our best to Mikey's mom."

"Cool," Porter said, and I could tell he was reading Steel's text, judging by the wicked gleam in his eye. "And I'll get back to Steel."

"Be nice," I said, shooting him my well-practiced *don't be a dick* look.

"As if I would ever not be nice," Porter said with a snicker as his fingers began furiously tapping away.

I didn't want to be a dick myself, but I had to admit, Steel's text did amuse me. Let's just say, Nick was being a major handful and giving him a hard time, testing the boundaries of their relationship in lots of ways. Steel was a very experienced Daddy, and he'd even played with little before...but Nick was not your average boy, and as things were shaping up, not your typical little either.

I knew they would be able to work it out in the end, but those two were definitely going through some interesting stuff.

"So, it's just you and me tonight then," I said.

"Yep," Porter said, finishing off his text to Steel. "The two last single Daddies standing."

I *hmpfed* into my lemonade and looked out the window,

watching the parade of hipsters and eccentric, yet moneyed and stylish people who had created their own slice of bohemian heaven in what was known as Daylesford's Vegetable Packing District.

Even in a place like this, with its mix of eclectic and out-there people, I still felt like I didn't belong.

There was mainstream, which was where most people fit in.

Then there was the alternative, a smaller group of people who rejected the mainstream.

But what if you didn't fit into either camp? What if you were somewhere on the sidelines?

"So," Porter said, putting down his cell phone and turning his full attention on me. "Tell me all about what's going on with you and Liam. And Hudson, please leave no filthy, sex-ravaged, explicitly sumptuous stone unturned.

"I'm going to need something stronger," I said, looking at my lemonade.

"Why?" Porter asked with a surprised tilt of the head. He wasn't pretending to be innocent this time, he was asking genuinely.

I huffed as I brought the completely inadequate lemonade to my lips.

"Because," I said after taking a drink, "it's hard to talk to you about stuff like this."

"Stuff like what, exactly?" Porter asked and I definitely picked up on a testy undertone.

"Sex," I said, putting my drink down on the table.

"Wait, you're saying it's hard for you to talk to me about sex? Uh, Hudson, have we not known each other for the last twenty years? When it comes to sex, whether talking about it or doing it, you know I am *easy*."

I appreciated his attempt at humor, but I ignored it.

"You're right," I said. "You're very experienced when it comes to sex. You're like the amusement park of kink, always up for a ride..."

I looked over at him and he was smiling, so I knew he was taking it the way I intended.

"Which is why I know you won't understand this. You won't get it."

"Try me," he said, slapping his hands down on the table in typical Porter style.

"If that's what you say to all the boys, no wonder you're so easy."

He let out a laugh and stood up. "I'm buying you a proper drink and then you're going to tell me whatever it is that you think I won't get."

It wasn't a question or even up for debate.

"Scotch?"

"Make it a double," I said.

"Coming right up," Porter said, turning to the bar before cheekily adding over his shoulder, "another thing that *easy* people say."

I smiled, but it faded quickly. With Stirling and Steel otherwise occupied, it really did leave only Porter to talk to about this. I did have other friends in my life, some guys from back in my weightlifting days, even a couple of guys from the gym that I was friendly with, but no one even came close to the original quad squad from college.

I sighed into my lemonade. I just knew that Porter wouldn't get it. I could feel it deep down. But I didn't have any other choice. I needed some advice, even if it was going to be well-intentioned but totally bad advice from the wrong person to be talking to about it.

Porter returned with my double scotch and sat down. He wasn't doing his overly excited schoolboy routine that he often did when the topic of sex came up. He was being strangely quiet, almost respectful. It was as if he could sense that, after twenty years, I was finally prepared to break down my walls and let him in on some very personal stuff.

"Thanks," I said, taking a sip of my drink.

"Don't mention it."

A warm smile flashed across his face and he shot me a friendly look. We both had the same light green eyes, but his were slightly smaller and narrower than mine...and had fewer wrinkles around them.

"I'm assuming this is about Liam," Porter said after what felt like an eternity of silence.

"No," I replied, almost immediately. "It's about me."

Porter nodded but didn't say anything else.

"This is difficult for me to say," I began, taking another sip of scotch. "But you know I've always hated how people just assume things about me based on my appearance."

More nodding. He knew exactly what I was talking about. Heck, he'd been making the same assumptions about me like everybody else had. Just because I had muscles, tattoos, and a shaved head, everyone assumed I was an alpha, a powertop, or a Dom. It was like they were the only options available to me.

But they weren't.

"I'm not what people think I am," I said.

Hearing myself say even those words for the first time stirred something within my chest. I couldn't tell if it was a good feeling or a bad feeling, all I knew was that more scotch was very much needed. I took a swig before continuing.

"I'm not an alpha powertop Dom, or some combination of any of that," I said.

"Oh."

"And I'm not a bottom or a sub either," I said, guessing where his mind was likely going.

"Oh."

I could see Porter's pupils dilate in shock as he shuffled in his seat. I guess I had just blown twenty years of assumptions out of his head. He remained quiet and I had to admit, I was liking the restraint he was showing.

Maybe it was better that Stirling and Steel weren't here. This quieter, stripped back version of Porter wasn't half bad.

"I've always felt a little different when it comes to sex," I said.

"Different, how?" Porter asked delicately.

"I don't know." I took a moment to collect my thoughts. "It's not that I don't enjoy the act of sex, it's just that for me it isn't the be all and end all that everybody makes it out to be, you know? And I don't mean that as a dig at you Porter, I really don't."

"I know you don't," he said amicably. "Go on."

"So yeah, sex wasn't this amazing thing that I had built it up in my mind to be. So of course, I thought that it meant that I was completely fucked up. Maybe I wasn't good at sex, or maybe I wasn't with the right guy, or maybe the guy I was with wasn't good at sex...I just kept running around and around in my mind with all of these unhealthy, shameful thoughts."

I took another sip of scotch before continuing.

"And then I met Richie. We were good in a lot of ways, but we were also incompatible in other ways. And one of those ways that we were incompatible was sex. By that point, I preferred topping to bottoming, so we were two tops in a relationship."

"Oh dear," Porter said, giving me a knowing look. "How did you guys handle it? Did you...?"

"Open things up?"

Porter nodded, almost a little sheepishly.

"We thought about it and we talked about it. A lot. We even went out one night, got insanely drunk and found a guy we thought we could have a threesome with. We were taking him back to our place when we both threw up in the car."

"Eww, not very sexy," Porter laughed.

"No," I said with an embarrassed chortle. "We just didn't want to go down that path. But we thought we had no choice. Until I discovered something very...unique."

"Oh?" Porter sat up a little straighter, his light green eyes zoomed in on me.

"You don't just have to be reduced to a convenient label," I said. "Sure, there are tops, there are bottoms, there are switches, but then, there are also...sides."

"Sides?"

"Yeah. I read an article about it a few years ago. I mean, yes it's a label as well, but it's a label for guys that don't fit into any of the other categories, basically."

"Um," Porter managed. He had a look on his face that I had never seen before. Speechless. "What else is there, Hudson? I've never heard of being a side before?"

"Well, there you go. You learn something new every day, Porter."

"What exactly is a side?" he asked. It sounded like he was either unimpressed or pissed. Or both.

"I can't speak to it broadly, I can only tell you what it means to me. And for me, sex isn't just about fucking. Penetration isn't my gold standard."

A moment of silence followed. Very uncomfortable silence.

Porter's face looked like he was in pain. Finally he spoke. "But you can't just say that, Hudson. You can't just change the rules of the game like that. Penetration *is* the gold standard of sex, whether you like it or not. Your opinion doesn't matter."

My jaw clenched.

"Why not?" I said defensively. "If one type of sex doesn't work for me, why can't I just find and do and enjoy the other types of sex that do work for me? I'm not hurting anyone."

"Hey, don't get angry at me. I'm not being judgmental here. I'm just trying to understand, because this isn't normal."

"Normal?" I spat the word out. "Right, so now *that's* the gold standard we should all be aiming for, is it? *Normal*. And whose normal are we talking about anyway? You know, there are people who think that being a Dom isn't normal."

I knew I was hitting Porter below the belt with that one, but it was true.

The world wasn't all rainbows and unicorns, filled with progressive and accepting people. I watched the parade of all sorts of people pass by us outside. How many of them were really, truly open and accepting?

"Well, what do you do then?" he asked, hitting me right on my rawest of raw nerves. The same raw nerve Liam had unintentionally struck last night when he dismissed what we had done as '*not real sex*' without knowing that, for me, it was.

It infuriated me that people reduced sex to just fucking, when there was a whole other world of things that two—or more—people could do together. There was an almost endless list of sexual activities that didn't involve penetration—masturbation, oral sex, rimming, frotting, kissing—and each of them came with a multitude of their own variations.

For me, my connection to another person was expressed mainly through mutual masturbation and, sometimes, oral sex. My desire for those acts was just as real as Porter's desire for fucking ass. So why was I the freak here? Why was I the one under the microscope, having to defend what I liked, as well as what I didn't?

I stared blankly at Porter, trying my best to walk myself off the mental ledge I was on. My body was flooded with years of pent up shame, guilt, and...even rage. Why did me liking what I liked, depend upon the approval of others?

More importantly, why did I let other people's lack of approval affect me so much?

Because you're destined to end up alone.

Those were Richie's words from one of our most heated arguments. They pierced through my walls and lodged themselves deep in my gut. Maybe I really was a freak and was going to end up all by myself, unable to find a guy that would want to be with me, a guy who would think that I was enough.

"I'm going now," I said after I gulped down the rest of my drink. I wasn't going to dignify his question with an answer. It was beyond insulting and had hurt me deeply.

"You know, you can be a really insensitive asshole sometimes, Porter."

And with one final look of disgust, I stormed out of the bar.

CHAPTER SEVENTEEN

LIAM

"This is such a good idea. I don't know why I didn't come up with it earlier," I said as I pressed up against Hudson and took the most perfect couple selfie. "You look amazing in a tank top, by the way."

I smiled as I began to apply the finishing filters and touches to the photo. I could have added in a tuxedo or raggedy old white shirt too. It didn't matter what the man wore, he made it look damn good.

I mean, he owned a gym. He worked out every day. I may have stopped training with him, but I did enjoy stopping by and saying hi on my way to the studio. When I walked in and saw him standing behind the front desk, the same desk he'd stood at when I first walked into the gym that night, I felt a giddy euphoria.

He did something to my insides and it made me think things I'd never thought about.

Sexual thoughts.

Like what his hands would feel like as they explored every inch of my body. Would he be gentle, or would his calloused hands be rough against my skin? Would he take his time, or would he be too hungry to take it slow?

What would it feel like to unbutton his pants and take his cock in my mouth? How would I feel on my knees in front of the man, worshipping his cock?

I'd never ever had thoughts like that before. It was like I'd had a filter in my brain that stopped me from going there. Anytime I would see an attractive guy, I'd think to myself *he's hot*, but that would be it. There'd been no imagining or endless daydreaming about fucking him or even seeing him naked.

And I always felt like that part of me was defective and needed fixing. I mean, sexual desire is normal. Everyone else seemed to have it, except for me. I hardly ever got aroused, and I certainly never got excited by anyone the way I did by Hudson.

And since our conversation last week at his place, the one where I thought he wanted to end things because he didn't like me, I was on a high. Because now I knew for a fact that Hudson Madden liked me.

He really, really liked me.

It felt stupid and dorky and oh-so-cliched, but I didn't care. I was like a schoolboy who was starting to fall...for the first time.

Was it possible to be crushing on someone who had a crush on you?

Holy hell, when he had told me that, with gentleness in his eyes, I was as shocked as a Texan farmer in a snowstorm.

And I knew that we hadn't technically had sex, but in a weird way, it was enough for me. More than enough actually. I mean, I had never come twice in a row before. I hadn't even thought it was physically possible for a man to be able to do that.

For as long as I could remember, I'd felt weirded out by sex. The very few times that I had fooled around with guys, it produced anxiety instead of arousal within me. There was more dread than desire flowing through my body. I did it, I went through with it, and it was okay, but it felt more like I was just going through the motions than anything else.

But with Hudson?

That was completely not the case. I didn't know how he managed to do it, but he took the anxiety or dread that I had previously felt and gently lifted it off, before it even had a chance to wrap itself around me.

He made me feel at ease, but more than that, he filled me with a deep yearning. For him, as well as for sex in general. I wanted his hands exploring my body, opening me up to pleasurable sensations I didn't even know were possible.

I glanced up from my phone at Hudson. He looked a little uncomfortable. I figured it was just the crazy posing I had subjected him to for the last ten—okay, maybe fifteen—minutes.

Even though this was his gym, he probably felt a little self-conscious posing with a local weatherman out on the gym floor in front of a full-length mirror, for the entire world to see.

"You okay?" I asked.

"Yeah, fine," he said, sounding distracted. "I think we've just had a walk-in enter. I need to go."

"Oh, sure, of course."

I leaned up for a kiss, but nothing. Hudson walked past me and hurriedly made his way to the front desk. I brushed it off. He was working after all, and I was bothering him with something as stupid as trying to get some extra publicity before the local media awards.

The stupid awards that were coming up faster than my hair was growing. I was still just short of three and a half inches, which explained why Parker was frantically scouring the internet for all sorts of weird and wonderful herbal concoctions to make hair grow faster.

I shuddered at the thought of the upcoming awards. They were Daylesford's night of nights. I knew how important they were for my promotion. If I won the best local weatherman award again, making it four straight years, Parker thought I'd be a lock for the promotion, and could even be shipping out to New York City as soon as the following week.

The thought of leaving was what made me shudder.

Of leaving...Hudson.

He was the first person I'd ever met who accepted me. He found the real me, the one underneath my public persona, interesting and valid. I was someone he wanted to get to know better. There was something freeing and wild about that. It made me do insane things like straddling him and letting him jerk me off.

Just the fact that I had the urge to do that, and then the guts to follow through on the impulse and actually do it, was a massive thing for me. He made me feel so safe and wanted, which released the parts of me that I'd always thought were bad and unlovable. They were still there, and maybe they always would be. But I was starting to see that I could learn to live with them, and still explore my sexuality and my desires.

And I wanted to keep doing that...with Hudson.

It may have been my idea not to use labels to define what was happening between us, but I was already starting to regret that. I'd inadvertently given Hudson an out, and it meant that I wouldn't find out just what sort of unconventional things he was into. That forced my imagination into involuntary overdrive...and I felt the all-too-familiar anxiety and dread.

Because, I think I knew what he was talking about when he said he was unconventional. I mean, it was kind of obvious. Everyone who looked at him saw a beast of a man. He was tall, wide-shouldered, and packing three hundred pounds of pure muscle. Add in the tattoos and the shaved head, and it was pretty clear what most people thought of him.

He was an alpha male.

A strong Daddy.

A total top.

So, if you flipped that on its side, what did you get?

I had been racking my brain about it almost non-stop for the past few days. Eventually, it became so crystal clear that I wondered how I hadn't seen it earlier.

Porter was unconventional because, for a man who looked the way he did, he was actually submissive. That had to be it. There weren't really any other options.

It explained why he wanted to avoid talking about it so much. He was probably used to people judging him, and worse yet, maybe even rejecting him for it.

I would never do that. I'd been rejected by guys before when I wouldn't go any further with them. To be made to feel bad when you simply stated a preference or a limit was one of the most awful feelings in the world. I would never subject Hudson to anything like that. He could tell me anything, even that he was a submissive bottom, and I wouldn't judge him for it.

I knew a thing or two about being judged simply based on the way I looked. With my stupidly large ass, everyone assumed I was a power bottom, but I wasn't. Nor was I a top.

No, I was just an incredibly inexperienced twenty-seven-year-old virgin whose best sexual experience so far had been a handjob a few days ago at the hands of the man now standing over me.

"Hey," I said, looking up.

"Hey yourself." He shot me a bright smile and I felt relieved that whatever had been bothering him earlier, seemed to have resolved. "You know," he continued, "I'm not the only one that looks good in a tank top."

My eyebrows shot up. And for one of the first times in my life, so did my cock.

Holy shit, how was the man able to do that with just a few words, a smile, and his booming presence?

"Would you be interested in, uh, coming back to my place?" he asked as his cheeks filled with the customary rosy blush I never got tired of seeing.

Hell yeah.

The slight hesitation in his question drove me all sorts of crazy.

I loved it when this big, burly beast of a man showed me some of his vulnerability, his softness. There were so many more layers to him, and I wanted so badly to unpeel them and get to know him better. All of him. Whatever unconventional things he was into, I would be fully supportive.

"Sure." I flashed him a wide smile.

Relief flooded his face, and as he grabbed me by the hand, the warmth of his fingers spread through my entire body. That thing that he did to me was happening again.

Desire was surging through my veins, along with relief. I was glad that I was able to even experience desire. For so long, I'd thought I was broken and defective for not being able to.

Now I was beginning to see that there was nothing wrong with me. Even if I had gone my whole life without experiencing desire or attraction, I would still have been normal and loveable and totally unbroken. For some people, that's just not what they want or need.

But meeting Hudson awoke some part of me. He lit a spark deep inside that was causing embers of desire to pop up all over my body. It was sexual. It was physical. But it was more than that too.

I felt giddy as we made our way out of the gym. For the first time in my life, a red-hot desire was embedded in every thought, every feeling, every cell of my body, and I knew exactly what I was chasing.

I wanted Hudson Madden with every fiber of my being.

CHAPTER EIGHTEEN

HUDSON

I'd been a bit hot and cold with Liam over the last few days, because I was feeling a little bit hot and cold with myself.

Porter had pissed me off, no doubt about it. The sad truth was, it wasn't the first time I had gotten that kind of reaction from a guy before. It was all too common to be dismissed as *less than,* or as if somehow my feelings, desires, and attractions weren't real. They may not have been common or easily relatable for a lot of people, I got that, but they were as real as the sky was blue for me.

Instead of feeling or being restricted because I was a side, I felt freer and more true to myself than ever. I wasn't limiting myself by not having penetrative sex, I was exploring and opening myself up to new worlds of pleasure, sanctuaries that, in some ways, were beyond the reach of guys who thought that fucking was the be all and end all of sex.

And that had a lot to do with what I had been studying over the last eighteen months. While I had told my friends, and Liam, that I was interested in pursuing psychology, I had already begun studying something else.

Tantra.

For me, tantra was like a bridge linking the physical, the mental, and the spiritual aspects of sex together so beautifully. It was never about a sexual position or a label, it looked at the totality of a person—who they were, what they wanted—and met them right where they were. It was never limiting, and just as importantly, it was never a judgment or an indictment on any sexual practice or behavior.

It also introduced me to out-of-this-universe pleasure beyond anything I could have ever imagined. If Liam thought that making him come twice in a row was an achievement, I couldn't wait to see his face when I introduced him to multiple waves of orgasms that seemed to go on forever. But we'd need to work up to that with a lot of breathwork, edging, and practice. Countless hours of practice.

In some ways, discovering tantra had helped heal me after Richie's death, showing me beauty and love at a time when all I felt was anger and despair. It sustained me and gave me hope that, even if I were to spend the rest of my life alone, I could still find beauty, pleasure, and sexual release all by myself.

It connected me to other people in deeper and more profound ways. And it wasn't just about sex. I felt a deeper empathy and compassion for everyone I encountered. Most times without them even realizing it.

Which was why I was starting to get sick of being rejected for being a side, and sick of hiding that I was interested in tantra. There was nothing wrong with me, and I was still angry at Porter for trying to make me feel that there was.

Liam had made me feel bad too, but he had done it unintentionally, so I wasn't mad at him about that. His comment about what we had done not being real sex was, unfortunately, just something that most guys said. I got it. For most guys a handjob was something they did quickly in the shower, or under the sheets at night. Alone and as a second-rate substitute for sex.

Same went for oral sex. A blowjob was usually considered either foreplay leading up to the main event, or something you did in a relationship, on the way to the real thing. Second base, or was it third base? Hey, I lifted weights, I didn't play baseball.

The second we got inside my place, Liam was on me, his warm body pressed against me, his lips hungrily biting my neck.

"Same as last time?" he said with a devilish look in his eyes.

I scooped him up in my arms and grunted, taking him up the stairs and into my bedroom. His body bounced against mine and I knew that tonight would be the night where I would tell him everything about me.

But first, I had a plan to make him come...three times. At least.

In addition to crowning, I wanted to take my time and edge him a little more. It was important to build up resilience, and edging was a great way to ward off coming too soon.

I wanted to lavish his cock with increasingly firm, deep strokes, building the pressure within him, then encouraging him to not release it, but instead to ride the wave. That would involve introducing him to breathwork, which I had a feeling he would pick up pretty quickly.

And then maybe I'd throw in the corkscrew right at the end.

I rubbed my hands in delight as we walked into the bedroom, and I gently lowered him onto the floor.

This was going to be good...

The rocking and spasming started to subside, making way for the occasional twitch. Liam's body finally settled on gentle rounds of occasional light trembling. It was a thing of beauty to witness Liam climbing the mountain, reaching the peak, and exploding three times, before climbing back down the mountain.

Back to himself.

Back to me.

"Ahhhh." His eyes were still fluttering as the sound escaped from his lips.

I ran my hand over his forehead, gently scooping up the beads of sweat that had formed. It was common to be this depleted, especially after coming three times, and especially when it was someone's first time.

He was slowly coming back to Earth, but I had no intention of hurrying him. He had no idea how beautiful he looked, or how much it filled my entire being with joy and happiness and love to be so close to him like this. So connected.

"Whoa," Liam croaked.

I handed him a glass of water. "Here you go, have a drink."

Liam shuffled up a little higher, took the glass in his still trembling fingers, and chugged it down.

"Looks like you worked up quite the thirst there."

"You have no idea," he said, dropping the glass into my waiting hands. "Holy...holy...holy..."

"Stop that." I smiled. "You're making me feel like I'm in church."

He tried to laugh, but it came out as more of a splutter. The most adorable splutter I had ever heard.

"What was... How did you... How did I...?" Words were still clearly eluding him.

"Just relax." I gently guided him a little lower in the bed so he could lie down. I lay down next to him, facing him. I grazed the back of my fingers up and down his tender, rosy cheek.

We lay there, in our own little mushroom cloud of blissed-out happiness, for a good while. I never wanted it to end, and I had a feeling that Liam didn't want it too either.

"I've never experienced anything like that, Hudson. Well, not since the last time I was with you."

His warm breath washed over my face and it felt divine.

"You're welcome," I said. I was beaming with pride at his words. "What did it feel like for you?"

"I don't even think I can put it into words."

"Try," I prodded as his gray eyes met mine.

I wanted to know. I had to make sure before I told him.

"I felt...connected. Aware. I was very, very aware of what was happening to my entire body, not just my cock. When you grazed your fingers over my stomach or my thighs, I felt it. When I curled my toes when I came hard the first time, I felt it. When my heart felt like it would explode out of my chest when I came the second and third times...I just felt it all."

He opened his mouth to speak again, but hesitated. Then, as if giving himself a mental nod of encouragement, he said, "And I felt...you."

"Me?" I asked, a little surprised.

"Yeah, you," he replied, smiling as if it were the most obvious thing in the world.

He grabbed my fingers and pressed them to his lips.

"No one has ever made me feel like this before. I didn't think..." He swallowed a few times, hard. "I didn't think that someone like me could ever feel like this."

"I'm so glad to be able to share this with you," I said as I traced my fingertips over every single crevice of his lips, feeling the smooth, sweet wetness of him. "Do you remember last time when we did...this...you said it *wasn't really sex?*"

His whole body stiffened. "Hudson, I'm sorry. I didn't mean..."

I pressed my fingertips more firmly against his lips. "Let me finish. Please."

He remained stiff, but nodded for me to go on. I could feel my heart thundering in my chest, but I knew it was the right time. I had to tell him.

"Well, for me, what we did then...and what we did just now...this is real sex. This is as real as it gets for me."

A wrinkle formed on his forehead. I dragged my fingers from his lips, up his nose, and along the ridge of the wrinkle.

"Liam," I said, drawing on the well of internal strength I had spent the last several years building up. "I'm a side."

"A side?" he asked. There was curiosity in his voice, but not even the slightest hint of judgment.

"I've taken some time over the last few years to work on myself and figure out what it is that I really and truly want. I've always been a sexual person, but for some reason, full-on sex, just doesn't...sit right with me. I tried it, of course. Topping, bottoming, but it just isn't for me."

Our eyes met and there was genuine affection there. I could feel it.

"But this...touching, kissing, hands, mouths, exploring bodies, communicating silently, more deeply...this is what I like to do. It's all that I like to do, when it comes to sex. Penetration doesn't feel right to me, it doesn't click into place like it does for other people. For me, this is what feels right."

I let out an almighty exhalation. There, I'd done it.

I'd shown him who I was, and now, I'd told him who I was. At least when it came to sex.

I looked at Liam. He had come down off his epic post-orgasm high, but he still had a light, floaty quality to him.

I couldn't tell what he was thinking or feeling.

Part of me was petrified that he would laugh at me and leave, like so many men had done before. That he would invalidate me by telling me that what I liked was weird and that it wasn't enough because it wasn't really proper sex. Or that he might...

"It feels so right for me too, Hudson."

Wait, did he just say that or was I dreaming?

"It does?" I asked, to make sure I wasn't hearing things.

He nodded and I could see his gray eyes darken with tears, looking like clouds that were about to burst.

"Yes," he whispered. "I never thought I could feel something like this. That I would want to, or that it was even possible. I felt so broken and so...wrong. But you've made me feel so right."

"Oh, really?" I said, wrapping my arms around him. The feeling of his skin pressed against mine sent shivers through my body. "I thought you were Mr. *I'm Always Right* Wright?" I grinned cheekily.

"Hold me closer, Hudson."

Liam's need to be held overtook him.

I did as he wanted, lifting him up a little and pulling him into me as close as possible. I stroked the back of his head. I could feel his heart pounding against me, racing a million miles a minute.

"What—what is this thing that you do? How do you make me come so much?" he asked as his heart rate slowed.

"It's tantra, Liam," I said, pressing a kiss into his forehead. "And it's one of the most amazing things in the world."

He pulled away from me to look me in the eyes.

"Will you show me more?" There was excitement mixed with nervousness in his question.

"Of course," I replied.

"Everything that you've said, everything that you've shown me so far, has just been so incredible..."

"And guess what?" I interrupted. "That's only just the beginning."

"It is?" His eyes practically fell out of his head.

I let out a laugh. "Oh, my sweet boy, it is. You have no idea the world of pleasure that awaits us."

"Like what?" This time, it was just pure excitement in his voice, with no trace of nervousness.

"The things we can do to each other. The heights of pleasure we can soar to..."

"I want you to teach me everything," Liam said with both conviction and desperate urgency.

"I want that too," I replied just as strongly.

Liam's mouth crashed into my neck, biting down hard and

catching me by surprise. His hands slid down my smooth chest until they found my nipples. My *incredibly sensitive* nipples.

"Ah," I groaned as his fingers tweaked and teased them ever so gently. My cock sprang to life at the unexpected turn of events.

I thought we would talk some more, maybe get some food delivered and just chill for the rest of the evening. It was a lot to take in, and I knew Liam had an avalanche of questions to throw at me. But Liam didn't seem interested in talking right now.

And he was always right, after all.

So I surrendered to his touch, his exploration of my body. As I exhaled, it hit me that I'd never been with someone after I'd told them about being a side and my interest in tantra. This would be my first time being with a man who knew me...all of me.

"How many times can you come?"

"Why don't you let me show you?"

And with that, Liam peeled my pants down my legs. He kneeled over me, kneading his fingers against my cock straining through my briefs. It longed to be released, it ached for his touch.

Liam was in no hurry, looking like he was enjoying taking his time as he ran his fingers over my bulge, the same way he traced them along my arms when he was studying my tattoos. I moaned impatiently and was met with a sly smirk.

Oh, he knew exactly what he was doing. And I loved it.

I decided to surrender my body, all of my control, to him.

I sank heavily into the bed as I felt his warm mouth encase my hard-on through my briefs. I looked down my body and could see the flames of desire in his eyes as he tenderly sucked around my bulge.

His eyes flicked up to meet mine. I wanted to bring him up next to me and kiss those sweet lips of his. But he was in control here, I reminded myself. And more than anything else, I wanted to see what he would do next.

I didn't have to wait much longer, as he tore the briefs down my legs and lunged at my already moist cock. He wrapped his lips around the head and took as much of me as he could.

The sight of him bobbing up and down on my cock thrilled me. His eagerness, his passion, his hunger awakened something in me, something that had been untouched for so long.

Desire.

He was showing his want and need for me by the way he was worshipping my cock. He wrapped his fingers around the base and gave it a good squeeze, while he held my balls at the same time.

The pleasure and pain of it made me buck my hips with excitement. He stuck his tongue out and played with my glistening slit, gently scooping up my precum and swirling it in his mouth.

"Is this okay?" he asked, his lips swollen and his voice rougher than I'd ever heard it.

"Oh, it is, my sweet baby," I said tenderly.

"I love your sweet lips wrapped around my cock. I might like to come, let's say, five times tonight."

His eyes practically fell out of his head, but he didn't miss a beat. My cock was down his throat quicker than I could let out a groan.

I smiled as I let myself be taken by Liam.

CHAPTER NINETEEN

LIAM

"I'm feeling nervous, Parker," I said, pacing up and down the hectic backstage area of the Daylesford Local Media Awards Night. People with headsets and clipboards were buzzing around us like flies, yelling directions and working their asses off to make sure everything went smoothly onstage.

"Can you please stop pacing?" Parker said, grinning. "You're making *me* nervous. Here, sit down."

He patted his hand onto the hideous green vintage couch he had perched himself on.

I slumped down in the chair next to him as carefully as I could. I'd already gone through hair and makeup, so I didn't want to mess my look up. Especially my hair, my perfectly primped and styled three-point-six inches of hair.

The red carpet had gone smoothly. The award organizers had decided to go for a more subdued experience to reflect the shitshow times we were living in. The red carpet was replaced with black carpet in honour of Black Lives Matter, and *Truth Wins* and *Facts Are Facts* signage provided a sombre, yet elegant backdrop for photos.

My date for the evening was my Daddy, of course. I clung to his arm, glowing with exhilaration and feeling on top of the world. To the outside world, we looked like a typical, happy couple who were just starting to fall in love. All very sweet and all very Mrs. Langley approved.

But we were creating our own amazing, intricate, spiritual, only-us world. Over the past two weeks, Hudson and I had explored each other's bodies, and our own, with such unrestrained joy and abandon, that just standing with the man, hand-in-hand as we faced the cameras, set off fireworks in my belly.

I was beyond happy.

I felt like I was walking on air.

I never wanted it to end.

Parker's cell phone went off like an explosion. It was met with a tsunami of head-snapping and looks of derision.

"All cell phones are to be switched off," a bitchy-sounding male voice yelled out from somewhere.

"Sorry, sorry, sorry," Parker said, waving his hand in the air apologetically. He looked down at the screen and then back to me. His eyes went wide. "It's them."

He got up and practically raced to find a quiet spot to take the call.

I leaned back against the couch. Parker was so sure I would get the promotion, he had even developed two theories about when I'd receive the offer call.

Theory number one was that I would get the call after the awards show, but that it would be dependent on whether I won or not. That theory was based on national not being one hundred percent sure about their decision, and wanting to test my viability and popularity. A win would mean I got it, a loss would mean they'd go with whoever was their second choice.

Theory number two saw them calling and making the offer before the awards. If they did that, it would be a sign that they were sure about me and didn't need some local media awards to verify their decision.

We'd both been tense all week, waiting for that call. When it hadn't come, I took it as a sign.

National was waiting to see how these awards played out. They weren't entirely sold on me, even after every goddamn trick we had pulled to get as much publicity and popularity as possible.

When I'd looked at Hudson in the limousine as we made our way to the awards and felt like my chest expanded infinitely at just the sight of him, I took that as a sign too.

I was falling for Hudson Madden in a very big way.

When Hudson told me he was a side, it felt like his words were unlocking parts of me that I'd never known existed. They were parts of me that I had buried deep, and covered with layers of shame, guilt, and fear.

I thought there was something wrong with me for not wanting sex twenty-four seven like almost every single red-blooded guy seemed to.

I felt embarrassed by being a twenty-seven-year-old virgin, and secretly, being fine with it and in no hurry to pop my proverbial cherry.

And I'd felt broken when I did have sexual experiences with guys, but they just didn't do it for me. It left me feeling cold and disconnected.

With Hudson, though, I wasn't feeling any of those things.

It was the best possible kind of surprise. I had learned that, even though I wasn't interested in being a top or a bottom, I still had a healthy, even voracious, sexual appetite. I simply needed to find different ways to channel and express it.

Hudson was showing me ways to do that.

By slowing things down and really taking it all in, I was connecting to my entire body, from the top of my head to the tips of my toes. He could set it all alight with just a touch, a lick, a rub.

He was patient with me and guided me through the journey. I was discovering my own body almost as if for the first time. I never knew that my inner thighs were so sensitive to touch.

I never realized that it felt nice to have a tongue lapping around my armpits. It tickled a little, but it turned me on too.

I had never experienced having the skin just above my hip bone gently grazed, which made me leak precum like crazy.

I had never noticed that when I came, I groaned loudly and deeply. It was a guttural, primal sound. Previously, I'd always been embarrassed to hear myself making any sounds of sexual pleasure. But Hudson encouraged it, he wanted it...and somehow, he made me want it as well.

And I loved seeing his body too. There was something so erotic in seeing this giant beast of a man handle himself, his thick cock in his hands, with a familiarity and a sense of reverence.

Everything he did was deliberate, mindful, and connected.

He didn't just stroke his cock furiously to get himself hard. He took his time, trying out all sorts of hand positions that I'd never seen before, focused purely on pleasure and doing what felt right, not doing what had been done a million times before.

When he explored my body with his tongue, it was as if he were picking up on all the cues I was giving him without realizing I was doing it.

When he was kissing me, it felt like he was learning something about who I was at the same time.

The world we were creating was so beautiful and romantic and raw. It left me wanting nothing else.

"You got the promotion," Parker said, running up and crashing down on the couch next to me.

He grabbed my hands and shook them excitedly.

"You got the promotion," he repeated, in case I had missed it the first time. "Starting two weeks from now, you are going to be *Wake*

Up America's newest weather team member. They are going to put that thirty-nine-year-old weatherman out to pasture before you get there, and then the third morning hour will be all yours, Liam. We've done it. We're moving to New York!"

He flung his arms around me, bringing my face forcefully against his shoulder.

My colorless, lifeless face.

As much as I had wanted this for so many years and worked so hard to get it, hearing the news didn't bring me the elation I had expected it to.

Instead, it tore me in two.

I couldn't deny that part of it made me happy, because I had worked hard and I did want it on some level. But I also couldn't deny that leaving Daylesford and moving to New York would mean leaving Hudson, and I didn't want that—on any level.

Was I prepared to do that? Was I able to do that? Did I even want to do that?

"I take it this is a good thing then?" I said, still half squished into Parker's shoulder.

"Are you kidding me?" He pushed me away and grabbed me by the shoulders. "Liam, this is fantastic with a capital F. And it plays into my theory perfectly."

"How's that?"

"They called *before* the awards," he said, his voice ringing with excitement. "That's major. That means they really want you. It's not dependent on you winning some shitty local media award. They really, really want you. That means we have leverage and can definitely get them to get that tooth fixed for you as well."

"Uh huh."

What if I didn't want to get my tooth fixed?

"And," he said, smiling so widely that the lower half of his face was just teeth, "they want you to announce you're joining *Wake Up America* when you win."

I raised my hand and opened my mouth to protest.

"Don't worry, they've cleared it with KDR-9 management," Parker said, assuming that was what I was about to say.

"That's not it, Parker."

"Oh." Parker stilled and for the first time since breaking the news, looked at me properly. His nose scrunched up. "Liam, what's wrong? Why aren't you over the moon happy about this?"

An uncomfortable silence sprang up between us.

"What if I don't win the award?" I asked.

"You will, it's a done deal," Liam said with a dismissive hand wave. "These things are more rigged than any music awards ceremony."

"Oh...well, what if—what if I don't want to take the promotion?"

Parker's eyes met mine. We both froze, before he burst out laughing.

"Oh my god, Liam. You had me there. For a minute, I actually thought you were being serious."

Parker shot up off the couch, his fingers frantically tapping away at his cell phone, his face lit up like the sky on the Fourth of July.

"Parker," I said, getting up to stand beside him. "What about...Hudson?"

Parker looked up and tilted his head, looking like he was seriously thinking about it.

"Good point. Leave it to me. I'll come up with a good breakup scenario that makes both of you look good."

"No, that's not what I..."

Parker's phone rang and he picked it up.

"Hey, Tim, you heard? Yes, it's amazing news. You'll have to give me the lowdown on all the best places in New York. I want the best of the best. No wait, better than the best. I want the inside scoop that not even the A-listers have..."

His voice trailed off as he strode away, excitedly planning his future. Well, technically our future. So why did I feel like it suddenly didn't belong in my own life anymore?

It felt like somebody had their arms around my chest and was squeezing the life out of me. I took a few deep breaths to calm down. I had to get my mind settled enough to do what I had to do next.

I had to tell Hudson.

"Wright, your award is up next. Get to the side of the stage, please."

A sweaty-looking middle-aged man dressed in all black grabbed my lower back and pushed me to the side of the stage. Parker reappeared out of nowhere and grabbed my hand as we walked the final few steps to the edge of the main stage, hidden from view behind the massive curtains.

This was all happening too fast. I needed to speak to Hudson first. I knew I did, and it was what I wanted to do so badly, but I was being pulled under by a current that I couldn't swim out of.

"Now, remember," Parker said, squeezing my hand as we reached our mark. "Act surprised..."

That I could do.

"Be gracious and generous in your praise for everyone at KDR-9..."

That was no problem either.

"And then pause for the big announcement. Revel in it. It's your moment. Tell the world you're joining *Wake Up America*."

My heart was beating out of my chest, and my mouth was as dry as the Arizona desert.

"I need some water," I said.

"Water, we need water over here," Parker yelled, and out of nowhere, a water bottle landed in my hand. I opened it and gulped down half the bottle without breathing.

I could see the presenters reading through the nominees. I looked out into the darkened audience. Hudson was in the fifth row, but it was too dark to see him.

God, how I needed to see him, to speak to him, to hold him...before all of this happened.

"And the award for Daylesford's Best Weatherman is..."

Please don't be me, please don't be me, please don't be me.

"Liam *We Know He's Always Right* Wright."

Parker let out a squeal as he released my sweaty palm and gave me a gentle shove onto the stage.

The bright lights hit me and instantly my face lit up. It was a reflex, muscle memory pure and simple.

I collected the award from the presenters.

I waited for the applause to die down before launching into my well-rehearsed speech.

I thanked all the people I had to thank, including at the end, my wonderful boyfriend Hudson. I heard a couple of "awws" rise up in the darkened auditorium.

"And lastly," I said, overcome with emotion—sadness, not happiness, "I would like to announce that I will be embarking on an exciting new chapter of my life. Ladies and gentlemen, I am thrilled to let you know that I will be joining *Wake Up America.*"

The announcement was met with thunderous applause. I held the statuette up, mouthed one more thank you to the camera and then walked off the stage.

I felt sick to my stomach. The thought of Hudson, sitting there in the audience and hearing the announcement for the first time with everybody else, made me feel like I was going to throw up.

Was he ever going to speak to me again?

CHAPTER TWENTY

HUDSON

My stomach dropped to the floor as the words spilled out of Liam's mouth. At first I thought that maybe I had drifted off and woken up in a parallel universe. But that wasn't realistic.

Then I thought that maybe it was opposite day and this was, in fact, his way of saying that he was staying, and would never leave. But yeah, not super likely either.

I was panicking, searching for any other plausible explanation, desperate to avoid the only logical one.

Liam was leaving.

He was moving to New York, and he was going to leave me behind. Which, in all fairness to him, wasn't exactly a surprise.

After all, it was actually the reason why we had begun this fake relationship in the first place. It was just a shame that the time had come for this fake relationship to end.

He wanted that promotion to *Wake Up America* so badly, and our fake relationship basically guaranteed him everything he was after: tons of good publicity, a fighting chance at that promotion, and Mrs. Langley's approval.

In turn, I got some free promotion for the gym, which had actually worked. We were getting a ton of new enquiries and people joining ever since Liam had first tagged us, or whatever it was he did in all of his social media posts.

That was the deal. Plain, clear, and simple.

So why the fuck did it feel like someone had just poured acid down my throat? My fingers were wrapped around the sides of the seat so tightly that I thought I would break the goddamn thing. I shot out of my chair the second the applause rang out at Liam's announcement and made my way out of there.

I needed air. It was hard to breathe. Each clap felt like it was sucking up every last vestige of oxygen in the room. My chest was tight and my legs felt like lead. Walking, just plain, basic walking, felt like I was trying to make my way through quicksand, sinking deeper with each step.

I reached the end of the row I was seated in and bolted to the nearest exit. I pushed through the doors and made my way down the stairs, through the front entrance of the auditorium, finally making it out onto the street. The sound of cheering and clapping was replaced by cars driving past and people talking as they made their way down one of Daylesford's most popular boulevards.

I rested against a streetlight, trying to calm myself down, but I knew a storm was brewing within me. We'd had a deal, an arrangement. Was I expecting too much, thinking I'd be told about the promotion before he announced it to the whole fucking world?

That was the part I was stuck on, what really hurt the most. That he didn't even bother to tell me first. We hadn't seen each other much this past week, but he'd had plenty of chances to tell me. Heck, he even could have told me on the ride over to the awards.

But he didn't. Which could only mean one thing.

He didn't care.

I braced myself against the streetlight as the feeling of loss and being left behind overtook me. Liam didn't care about me. After everything we had talked about, experienced together, and felt...it didn't mean anything to him.

I winced, fighting against the tears that threatened to break through. I had lowered my walls and let him in, closer than any man I had ever let in before, and it didn't matter to him. He was only interested in the promotion, in advancing his career and getting the hell out of Daylesford.

My phone vibrated against my thigh. I fished it out of my pants and looked at the screen.

It was Liam.

"What is it?" I said bluntly.

"Hudson, where are you?"

It was hard to hear him with all of the noise in the background. It sounded like he was at a party. He probably was, his *congratulations on your promotion* party.

"I'm outside. I'm going home, Liam. Goodbye."

I hung up, but I couldn't disconnect from that word.

Goodbye.

There was nothing good about it.

I looked out at the busy street and tried to hail a cab. I must have been sending out foul vibes, because the cab gods were not smiling on me. After four or five failed attempts, I decided to just start walking. I figured a walk in the night air would give me a chance to think things through and clear my head a bit, so I set off.

"Hudson," Liam's voice rang out behind me.

I turned to see Liam running toward me, looking flushed in his tuxedo. His hair was flattened and messy. He was clutching the statuette in his hand.

"Hudson, wait up."

The sidewalk must have turned to wet concrete, because I froze. I knew I should have kept walking, but my legs betrayed me and kept me right where I was.

I wanted to ignore him and make him feel like he wasn't important, the way he had made me feel.

But I guess deep down, I just wanted to know...why hadn't he told me this himself?

He finally reached me and his scent blanketed me. I inhaled it for a brief moment, before the hurt and loss returned.

The sight of him—tousled hair, reddened cheeks, panting heavily—added kerosene to my emotions, and all of the sudden, I burst out in wild flames of anger.

"What the hell was all that about, Liam?" I raged at him, taking both of us by surprise. "Did you have any intention of telling me about this promotion before you let the whole fucking world know?"

"Hudson, it's not like..." he started, but I wasn't having it.

My anger wasn't going to be extinguished by some pathetic excuse or half-assed apology.

"Not like what, Liam? Huh? Not like me telling you the most private and personal things about me? I shared things with you that I've never shared with anyone else."

My voice was loud and rough, and given that we were on a busy street, it was drawing some weird looks from people walking past.

"Maybe we should talk somewhere else?" Liam suggested.

"Oh, what, now you decide that you want to talk privately, huh? But when you have something to say, it's fine for you to blurt it out to the whole world first?" I wasn't being reasonable, but I didn't care. I was wounded, and he was the one who had done it.

"Hudson, I'm sorry..." he began as tears started to fall down his face.

Then, suddenly, the sight of him looking so sad and so vulnerable doused the fuel of my fire. I stepped in toward him before stepping back again.

No, I couldn't let myself get sucked in...not again. I had already done that once with him, and look where it had gotten me.

I didn't know the reason for his tears, and part of me desperately wanted to. But another part of me knew that I shouldn't. There was no reason to know why he was crying, because there was no reason that could explain why he did what he did, other than what I already knew—he just didn't care about me.

So why was he crying? It kept gnawing away at me. But I had to let it go, just like I had to let Liam go. Not that I had any choice in the matter.

But still...his tears. Was there a part of him that was sad about leaving what we had behind?

I blinked that thought away. It was stupid, wishful thinking and nothing more.

Liam had announced he was leaving to the whole world. If he had any morsel of regret about it, he wouldn't have been practically crying with joy on stage as he was making the announcement. If he had any doubts about it, he had done a stellar job of keeping them from me.

Like the signage that had greeted us on the black carpet earlier had so clearly illustrated—*Facts Are Facts*. And the fact was, Liam was leaving and our fake relationship was over.

So was our *let's not put any labels on this* relationship.

"Porter was right about you," I said, wincing at the words coming out of my mouth. "I shouldn't have trusted you. You're selfish and you only care about yourself. Goodbye, Liam."

There was that word again.

Goodbye.

I turned around and heard Liam's cries behind me.

"Hudson, no...please don't go..."

I bit back the tears until I couldn't anymore. The warmth spilled down my face as I walked away from Liam.

The only man I had ever shown my true self to.

CHAPTER TWENTY-ONE

LIAM

"You know, you really don't have to help me with this, Parker. I can do it on my own."

Parker was taping up a box on the other side of my living room, which was filled with brown boxes and a sofa with two matching chairs, all waiting to go into storage.

Moving sucked.

It reduced my life to a mountain of boxes and a handful of items that were too big to fit into a box. It was depressing, or maybe I was just depressed.

"Hey," Parker said, looking up, his face lit up in a wide smile. "What would I rather be doing on a Saturday morning than helping the country's fastest-rising weatherman get ready for the next wild chapter of our adventure?"

I forced a smile. "I don't know, but maybe your Fleshjack is missing you?"

"Humor, I like it," Parker said warmly. "Better than moping and silence. And besides, my Fleshjack and I...well, let's just say we bonded intimately before I came over."

I picked up a pillow from the sofa and threw it at him. "I don't need to know the details, thank you very much. Besides, packing while moping in silence is the right way to do it. Packing sucks."

I looked around the room. One more box to go and then we were done in here.

"How's your packing going?" I asked.

We still had a week to go, but I had a feeling Parker had been packed and ready to leave the day after we got the news. Heck, he'd probably started packing the second he caught a whiff of the promotion.

"I'm all done," he said, sliding his fingers to secure the tape in place on the box. He got up and walked over to me. "Everything is packed except for the PlayStation...and the Fleshjack."

"Oh brother," I moaned.

"What's that box over there?" he asked, stepping past me into the hallway, where a lone box stood by the door.

"Oh..." he said as he approached it and saw *Hudson* scrawled in black marker pen across the top of it.

"Yeah, we haven't really talked about that yet, have we?" he said, turning back to face me. "Do you want to? Talk about it, that is?"

I shrugged. Not really. Maybe. Yes. I had no fucking clue.

"What's there to say, really?"

"Liam," Parker said, stepping back into the room. "I'm sorry."

"For what?" I asked, motioning to the only habitable part of the room, the sofa.

"For not realizing sooner," Parker said as he flopped down beside me. "It's my job to know pretty much everything there is about you, and this is a pretty big thing."

He had no fucking idea.

"Yeah," I conceded. "It kinda is."

"Talk to me," he said, bringing his knees to rest up under his chin. "Shoes on the sofa okay?"

"Yeah, fine," I said absently, my mind already drifting with thoughts of Hudson, and wondering how on earth I was going to be able to put any of those feelings into words.

But I tried.

I told Parker some stuff, keeping it relatively surface level. I acknowledged my feelings for Hudson had developed into something way more real than fake, and that we'd had a connection that I wasn't expecting. I told him that I felt something for Hudson that I had never felt for anyone before.

That was where I stopped myself. I had to. I was getting too close to the deeper stuff, the stuff I wouldn't dream of telling anyone about, not even Parker.

Like the way, for the first time in my life, Hudson made me feel like I was a complete and whole human being.

Or the way he understood me, and I got him too

Or the way we were totally, one hundred percent sexually compatible.

It might not have worked for anyone else. Heck, other people might have even looked at us and thought we were weird, but it didn't matter. We understood each other, what the other needed, and the desires we had. They were normal. They were natural. And they were beautiful.

And there was no way in hell I was telling Parker about the man's multi-orgasmic skills. Not only was that something that was super private, it wouldn't have been fair to make anyone else jealous like that.

"Okay, wow...that's a lot," Parker said, taking it all in once I was done talking. "Why didn't you tell me any of this before?"

I could hear the hurt in his voice.

"I didn't mean to keep this from you, Parker," I said truthfully. "I guess, it all just happened so unexpectedly. I mean, this was a crazy spur-of-the-moment idea to try and cook up some more publicity. It's not like I was spending hours on apps or at bars trying to find a guy."

Parker rolled his eyes at me.

"No one hooks up on apps or at bars anymore Liam," he said with a hearty scoff. "It's all happening on PlayStation."

It was my turn to roll my eyes at him.

"Seriously, CrazyCatDude48 and I have been talking, and I think we might grab a coffee next week."

There were times when I looked at Parker and realized just how little I knew him. This was one of those times.

"Oh shit." Speaking of time...I grabbed my cell phone and grimaced. "Dammit, I'm going to be late."

"Late for what?" Parker asked, but I could tell his thoughts were still on CrazyCatDude48.

"Hudson," I said with a heavy exhale. "We agreed to meet at his place at eleven so we could give each other our stuff back. You know, the stuff that we left at each other's houses to make it seem more real."

A flurry of emotions spun through Parker's eyes, like reels on a slot machine, until he finally landed on guilt.

He wasn't the only one who felt guilty.

I felt like the worst person alive for what I was doing to Hudson. It didn't feel right, but what could I do? I couldn't exactly say no to this promotion, it was a once-in-a-lifetime opportunity.

I wasn't getting any younger, and if I didn't take this chance now, I'd be destined to be a local weatherman for the rest of my life.

And really, did I want to be winning the *Daylesford's Hottest Derriere* award at the age of forty? Hmm...scratch that. I probably wouldn't even be in the running by that age, replaced by some younger, more attractive person. Just like what I was doing. A shiver ran down my spine at the ickiness of it all.

I let out a heavy sigh.

I knew I had to act now. However I approached it, there was no getting around the fact that my career clock was ticking, each passing year bringing me perilously closer to that dreaded cliff-edge of thirty.

This was my time. I had worked hard for it. I deserved it, and I wanted to take advantage of this opportunity.

Kinda.

Sorta.

I had to keep reminding myself.

As Parker and I made our way to the door, he grabbed me by the shoulder and said, "I know this must be tough for you. But remember why you're doing this, okay? I know you have bigger plans than just national. I know you want to grow your platform so that you can really make a difference and use your voice for good. Keep remembering that, okay Liam? That will help get you through this."

"Thanks," I said, giving him a quick hug before I picked the box up. It was good advice, but not even the best advice in the world could save me right now.

I had to go and face Hudson.

Somehow, I got into my car, drove over to his place, and ended up at his front door. How, I didn't even know, I was running on complete autopilot.

I lifted my knee, rested the box on it, and rang Hudson's doorbell.

As the *ding-dong* sound echoed in my head, it suddenly hit me this would be the last time I would ever see Hudson. A lump formed in the back of my throat as I tried to breathe deeper to steady myself against the sadness that was growing inside me.

"Hey," Hudson said as he opened the door, wearing a loose-fitting white shirt and gray sweats.

He kept his face neutral, and I couldn't help but notice the days of stubble lining his jaw and dark circles under his eyes.

"Hey," I said as normally and calmly as I could.

There was nothing normal or calm about this.

"Sorry I'm a little late."

"Don't worry about it." Hudson forced a smile as he let me in.

There was a brown box in his entryway. He closed the door

behind me, and all I wanted to do was drop the box I was carrying and fall into his arms. His massive arms that were so hard, and yet so soft at the same time. Those same arms that I had traced my fingers over, studying every intricate detail—every line, shape, and color—of the endless sea of ink that covered every inch of his skin.

"Um, here's your stuff," I said, handing him the box.

"Thanks," he said as he took it from me.

Our fingers touched. A fierce heat tore through my body with such ferocity I thought I would topple over. Onto him. Into those arms. God, how I wanted to be wrapped up in him again.

The entryway was a small-ish room, but it felt like we were standing at opposite ends of an empty sports stadium.

How could it all come to this? Would it really just end...like it had never even happened?

Would I wake up one day ten years from now and barely give a second thought to the decision I was making right now, or would I wake up ten years from now and kick myself for having made the biggest mistake of my life?

Something inside me screamed *yes, that, that right there. This is a fucking mistake. Wake up, Liam. Say something—do something— you idiot.*

But I couldn't say anything. I was powerless. Every time a word bubbled up in my throat and my lips opened, nothing came out.

I looked over at Hudson, into those beautiful light green eyes of his, and he looked as lost as I felt. I didn't want it to end this way, with my last memory being of a broken man.

A man that I had broken.

"Hey, I think I might have left one of your shirts upstairs. Let me go get it." Hudson took off before I could respond.

What was going through his mind?

I could see the hurt splashed across his face, and I assumed he was still angry at me—as he was completely entitled to be—but was there anything else going on with him?

Was there a part of him, even a small part, that wanted me to stay? Was he battling something within himself, wondering whether he should ask me not to leave? Or was he just angry at me, at this whole stupid situation that I had dragged him into?

I mean, his life had been perfectly fine before I walked into it late one night at the gym. He had his business, he had good friends, and he had a plan for his future. Maybe I'd just been an unwanted distraction for him?

Maybe in ten years time he'd wake up and that's what he'd think about all of this, that it was all just a silly game for a silly local weatherman to score some silly promotion.

That thought pinched my heart so much it hurt.

I could hear him thundering down the stairs, and I smiled. His bulky frame meant that the man did not move quietly. I could always tell where he was...and I liked that.

The memories of all the good things about the man filled me with the briefest happiness as he returned and threw my shirt into the box.

"You know, Parker said that as far as breakups go, this is a good one," I said in an attempt to try and make him feel a little better.

"Great," he grumbled.

Parker had come up with a good story. He had described it as a whirlwind romance, one filled with intensity, fun, and laughter...while it lasted. Unfortunately, due to conflicting work priorities, we weren't able to make it work. Those were the words from the article on page twenty-four of *The Daylesford Times*. The words that Parker had accidentally on purpose leaked to them. Words that didn't even begin to scrape the surface of the truth.

"Yeah," I said, trying desperately to inject some positivity into my tone. "Parker said that we'll both come out of it looking good. There's no bad guy, and it's kind of tragic enough to actually garner each of us some sympathy."

It was all true. The results of yesterday's testing confirmed it, but judging by Hudson's flat reaction, I didn't think he gave a crap about focus group testing.

"Great," he repeated. "Glad I could help."

He handed me the box, and this time, our fingers didn't touch. I missed it. I wanted it so badly, just a momentary graze of his fingertips against mine. I would have taken anything, even a small, incidental touch.

We looked at each other, neither one of us knowing what to say next.

I felt a single tear roll down my cheek, but with both hands on the box, there was no way for me to wipe it. Hudson saw it and his jaw twitched. For a moment, I thought he would move in and brush it away.

Instead, he just shuffled his feet and looked down.

"Well," I said with the sadness growing inside me. "I guess this is it."

"Yeah, I guess so."

"Goodbye, Hudson."

"Goodbye, Liam."

And just like that, I stepped out of his house and into my brand-new life without him.

CHAPTER TWENTY-TWO

HUDSON

As far breakups go, this is a good one.

The sour aftertaste of Liam's words hadn't diminished in the three weeks since he had said them.

A *good breakup* was like a *goodbye*...a complete and utter fucking oxymoron that left you feeling empty, confused, used, alone, and drinking scotch while watching morning shows. That was never a good thing.

In my defense, I had waited until the third hour, when Liam was on, to pop open my second bottle of the week.

Liam leaving tore me up way more than it should have, and way more than I was expecting it to. What we had was never even real, I had to keep reminding myself. We had called it a fake relationship right from the start, but even though the word fake was right there, it didn't feel fake to me.

Right from the beginning, it was like my dream had come true.

My crush walking into the gym late one night.

My crush being so much nicer, friendlier, cuter in real life than he was on TV.

My crush asking me out, and then to be his boyfriend. His fake boyfriend.

But it was what happened next that had me reeling.

I never expected to open up to him the way that I did. And I also never expected him to react as well as he had. He didn't judge, or criticize, or make me feel bad about who I was and what I liked.

In fact, he liked it. It actually worked for him. We were completely compatible in every way, especially sexually. I never thought I would get the chance to experience that with someone.

And for everything he didn't know, for every question he had, he was so open and receptive to letting me guide him.

That part of my Daddy instinct had never come out before. I'd had a vague feeling it was there, buried somewhere deep inside me, but I had never found the right guy to explore it with.

And I loved it. It ignited my soul in a way that was breathtaking. It was like I had found the core of what made me a Daddy, and was not only able to explore it, but encouraged and supported every step of the way.

Liam let me take the lead, guide him, and together, we explored not only each other's bodies, but our minds and souls as well.

"And now it's time for the weather," said a *way too perky for this time in the morning* female voice. I grabbed the remote and turned the volume up. "Liam, what's the latest on those storms making their way closer to Florida?"

"Thanks, Mary, I want to take you all straight to the tracker, where you can see the model showing us that this tropical storm has all the elements to turn into a monster hurricane."

I took a sip of my scotch as I settled back into the couch.

He was such a natural at it, born to do it. I couldn't begrudge him for chasing his dream. I just wished that I had been able to come along and share it with him.

I knew I had to stop doing this. Watching him every day wasn't healthy. But this was the inevitable aftermath of a good crush going bad.

Also, I had to stop listening to the song *Crush* by Jennifer Paige, which Spotify had added to my Weekly Discovery list. The only thing that song was crushing was my spirit.

Besides, I didn't want to go back to having a crush on Liam from afar. That would have been impossible anyway, after what we had been through together.

I threw back the last of the scotch as Liam wrapped up his last forecast for the morning. The alcohol scalded my throat in a too-familiar way. I barely felt it anymore. I put the drink down and picked up a piece of paper I had found when I was collecting all of Liam's stuff to give back to him.

It was the list I had started writing after my conversation with Liam at the gym, where I told him that his ass was my eighteenth favorite thing about him. I came home that night and, as I was tidying up the kitchen, I saw a piece of paper and a pen and I thought, *hey why not make a list of all the things I liked about him?*

I only added a few things that night, because I didn't really know him too well at that point. Eighteen things was a slight overreach, it was just the first number that popped into my head.

But over the time we spent together, I just kept adding to it, bit by bit, until I had filled it out in full. Hell, I could have kept going if...if *we* had kept going.

I read through the list for the millionth time.

I shouldn't have been doing that either. At some stage, I knew I'd have to throw it away...just not today.

18 things I like about Liam Wright:

- *He's the sexiest weatherman in Daylesford, no wait, the USA*
- *His jokes are funny, even if no one else thinks so*

- *He's adorable, especially when he's the only one laughing at his own jokes*
- *He never forgot about his brother, and he honors his memory so beautifully*
- *His crooked third tooth*
- *He's the Winner of Daylesford's Hottest Derriere—so, there's that*
- *Smart*
- *Kind*
- *Hard working and focused on his career*
- *The king of catchphrases*
- *Cuter in real life than on TV*
- *He's a virgin (he waited for me)*
- *He likes real talk*
- *He's comfortable with being vulnerable*
- *He cares about the environment*
- *He's patient*
- *He's sexually perfect—and just right for me*
- *He's going to make a difference and leave the world a better place*

I stared at the piece of paper, before crumpling it up and throwing it on the table.

"Fuck," I yelled out. I didn't want this pain anymore. I let my head fall over the back of my sofa and stared at the ceiling. I knew I had to get up and get over this. I couldn't keep wallowing in week after week of self-pity.

Nothing was going to bring Liam back, least of all sitting in my pyjamas, drinking scotch way too early in the day, and feeling sorry for myself.

I need to shower, shave, and maybe just leave my living room and go outside for a run or something. I couldn't even remember the last time I had done that. Just as I was about to get up, there was a loud knock on the door.

I looked down at myself and let out a sad sigh. My shirt was stained and smelly, and my *Finding Nemo* pajama bottoms weren't exactly designed for greeting guests at the front door. Oh well, it was probably just a delivery.

I opened the door and my eyes widened in surprise.

"Porter," I said. "What are you doing here?"

"Uhhh..." He inspected me like I was a science experiment gone awry. "I wanted to talk, but it looks like I may have to do an emergency fashion intervention first."

I pursed my lips, trying not to smile. I was still pissed with him and had been avoiding him since our fight. To his credit, he did try calling, and he had sent at least five apology texts afterward, but I had ignored each and every one of them.

"Can I come in? he asked. I could tell by his tone that he was unsure of himself.

I nodded and turned around. He followed me, closing the door behind him.

"Holy shit, Hudson, what the hell happened in here?" Porter said, eyeing my living room.

It may have been a little...messy. Okay, a lot messy. As in, there were piles of empty takeout containers and clothes occupying pretty much every surface, including the floor.

"Uh," I started, scratching the back of my neck sheepishly. "It's easier for me to find things?"

"Like..." Porter knelt down and picked up an empty scotch bottle. "...this?"

I sagged down onto the couch and shrugged. "I'll tidy up at some stage."

"This year?" he joked with a friendly smile as he sat down next to me.

"I'm still angry at you," I said, crossing my arms over my chest.

"Well maybe if you bothered to return my calls or answer any of my apology texts, you wouldn't be."

I growled at him, but there was no bite behind it.

Porter scanned the room one more time, before his gaze settled on me.

"I'm sorry, Hudson," he said.

I knew the man well enough to know when he was giving one of his bullshit, politician, non-apology apologies. I could tell that he was genuinely contrite.

"Really? Are you really sorry, Porter?" Just because I could see he was being genuine didn't mean I had to make it easy for him.

"I am, Hudson," he said in that voice that made me forgive him for pretty much everything he had done. "Your love life and your sex life is just as valid as anyone else's. I'm sorry that I made it sound like it wasn't. I was wrong to say that your opinion didn't matter. For saying that, and for hurting you, I apologize."

My heart lifted a little.

"Thank you," I said, giving his hand a squeeze. "And I'm sorry for calling you an amusement park of kink."

"That's okay," Porter said, brushing it off as if he'd been called worse, which, come to think of it, he probably had. "I'm sorry for calling you a tightly wound asshole."

"You never called me that," I said.

"Well, not to your face." Porter smiled sheepishly, suddenly looking like he was the one who needed a scotch before ten in the morning. "Are we friends again?"

"Hmm, I'll have to get back to you on that one," I said with a half-chuckle.

"I'll consider that a victory," Porter said, and just like that, all of his uncertainty lifted and he was back to his old self again.

"So," he said, turning to face me. "How are you going to get Liam back? I know it's going to be hard to top Nick's flash mob for Steel, but I'm sure that between the two of us, and however much scotch you've already had this morning, we can come up with an equally brilliant plan."

I smiled briefly at the memory of Nick's spectacular flashmob, but the smile abruptly disappeared from my face when I forced myself to face the realization that there was no grand gesture I could do to get Liam back.

Firstly, he wasn't really ever mine to begin with, and secondly, by the looks of how polished he appeared on TV, he was clearly loving where he was. Why would he come back to Daylesford and do local weather, just for me?

"Porter," I said, summoning up all of the remaining strength I had. I wanted to quell his enthusiasm before he got way too carried away.

"So," Porter spoke over me. "I've been doing a little research online. Here's what I've come up with."

The guy was like a freight train, completely unstoppable. I slouched further into the sofa, knowing I had little choice but to strap myself in and listen.

"It only costs a couple of grand to hire a whole bunch of hot air balloons to fly over Central Park. Then I was thinking, we could maybe dig through our playlists from college and see if we could get some '90s band who are desperate for cash to perform."

He didn't seem to be breathing, the torrent of words just kept pouring out of his mouth.

"Then we could set it up with the station for Liam to be doing a broadcast from Central Park. I've looked into it and it's possible to arrange to get some flyzone permits so that we can get you lowered down from a helicopter at the same time as the hot air balloons—"

"Porter!" I hollered. I'd finally had enough. "Stop. Please."

I pinched the bridge of my nose with two fingers.

"Look, I know you're only trying to help, and I appreciate it, but Liam is gone. And I have to accept it. I've got no other choice."

Porter studied me silently. I had stopped his grand romantic gesture fantasy mid-flight. I could see the remnants of excitement in his haggard breathing. Finally, he narrowed his eyes at me and nodded.

"Okay, if you're sure. If that's really what you want..."

It wasn't, of course it wasn't.

I wanted hot air balloons and helicopters and reunions live on national television in Central Park as much as anyone would have wanted those things. But none of it would change a damn thing. It wouldn't make even the slightest difference. Liam was never coming back.

"I'll respect your decision," Porter continued, "and I won't interfere."

"Whoa, don't go overboard there, Porter," I said teasingly. "I'm not expecting miracles."

He flipped me the bird as he laughed.

"Here's an idea. Why don't you go and get changed—because you look terrible—we clean this place up a little bit, and then you buy me, your last remaining single Daddy friend, lunch?"

"Deal," I said, getting up.

I really did need a shower, I was starting to stink.

"Hey, thanks, Porter, I appreciate this."

"No need to thank me. We're best friends, and Daddies always stick together."

He got up to stand next to me. "At this point, I would normally give you a hug, but you don't smell so fresh, my friend."

I laughed and didn't blame him in the slightest.

By the time I had returned, freshly shaved and smelling like my favorite wood-scented shower gel, Porter had made an impressive dent on the cleaning. One massive garbage bag was already full, sitting in the corner of the room, while he was busily filling up the second.

"Ah, that's better," he said when he saw me walk in. "You don't smell like a sewer anymore."

"Hey, I wasn't that bad." At least, I hoped I wasn't.

The time for moping and sulking and pity was over. Tidying up my living room was the first step I needed to take. My life would go on, and I would be just fine.

Somehow.

Even without Liam.

"Hey, no standing around and looking pretty," Porter said as a roll of garbage bags was flung across the room at me. I managed to catch them, tore a bag off, and began picking up whatever mess was closest to me.

"I want to get this done nice and quick, so that my best friend can take me out to lunch...at the most expensive restaurant in town. Hmm, do I feel like lobster or ribeye?" Porter said to himself, scratching at his chin in that annoyingly smug way of his.

I threw the roll of garbage bags back at him, but he managed to deflect it. I smiled and continued picking up my own mess.

At least my new life would start with a nice meal...even if I was the one paying for it.

CHAPTER TWENTY-THREE

LIAM

"And...we are done," the producer's thick Queens accent rang out loudly at the end of my segment. "Awesome work, Liam." He came toward me to unpin the mic from my shirt. "You're already a pro. Can't believe you've only been here a month."

I could.

"Thanks, Jim," I said as he freed me of the mic.

I made my way off the soundstage and into my broom closet of a dressing room. The joys of starting at the bottom...again.

Parker was already in there, pacing up and down, glued to his phone. Given the size of the room, and that he could only take a few steps before needing to turn around, I was surprised he wasn't making himself dizzy.

"Sit, sit, sit," he said when I entered, without looking up. "We have a lot to talk about."

I sighed. There was always a lot to talk about.

I slumped into the chair and looked at the reflection staring back at me in the mirror. I looked tired, faded. Even forcing a fake smile didn't help. Now that the network had paid for me to get my crooked tooth fixed, my smile didn't feel like my own anymore.

And that went for pretty much everything else in my life. Daylesford was a pretty big city, but it was absolutely dwarfed by the size of New York. Everything was so new and unfamiliar, and even though the streets were buzzing with excitement and energy, none of it felt like anything I wanted to be a part of anymore.

I was yearning to be back home.

And I missed Hudson so much that it fucking made my whole body writhe in agony.

The only good thing about the promotion had been that my stupid catchphrase was finally banished for good. The network liked it and thought it was cute and all...for local viewers, not a national audience in the millions.

I couldn't have agreed with them more.

Which was why Parker and I always had so much to discuss. He was constantly throwing a stream of ideas at me, to see if I would like any of them. After all, I was back at the bottom again, and the competition here was next-level cutthroat. If I wanted to work my way up the ranks and get a senior position, or maybe even a cushy weekend gig, I would have to work hard to stand out.

"What have you got today?" I asked, flashing him my best *this better be good* look.

He looked across at me and smiled. It was an uneasy look that made me nervous.

"Dick slip."

The words felt like a slap across my face. I shook my head as I looked at him to see whether he was being serious.

"What?"

"Dick slip," he repeated. "Accidental, of course."

I groaned, not liking where this was going.

"You're out on the weekend, jogging through central park, looking like the picture of American perfection that you are."

I grumbled some more.

"The sun's shining, you're smiling your new-and-improved smile, looking all fit and healthy until you have to tie up a loose shoelace, and low and behold, your dick pops out of your training shorts."

"Next," I said dismissively. There was no way in hell I was going to do *that*.

"No problemo." He returned to his clipboard and flicked a page over.

"Apparently the network is shopping around an idea for a reality TV show. The premise is a bunch of sexy, single New Yorkers looking for love...while cooking exotic dishes...completely naked."

"Next," I cried. I may have wanted attention, but I wasn't desperate enough to lower myself into the realm of reality television.

"Is this really the best you got, Parker?" I asked, giving him a half-stern, half-bemused look.

"Well, yeah," he admitted sheepishly.

I focused on his face. He scrunched his nose up, before taking off his glasses.

"I'm sorry," he began. "I've met someone, and I guess it's been taking up too much time. I've clearly lost focus here. It won't happen again, Liam."

"Hey, I love that you've met someone, Parker. You don't have to apologize for that. At least, not to me."

Parker looked up and squinted at the smirk on my face.

"What do you mean?" he asked.

"Well, I don't mind that you're seeing someone. But what about Fleshjack? Have you considered how this will affect your relationship with him?"

Parker threw his head back and let out a roaring laugh.

"Believe me, Liam, nothing will affect that relationship. Men come and go, but a Fleshjack lasts forever...or at least until a newer, more advanced model comes around."

I grinned as I looked at him. He seemed to be taking to New York City and his new life here like a duck to water. I was glad he was interested in someone. It was nice to see, but it also made it even clearer, just how much it wasn't working out for me.

Which was a pretty darn depressing thing. This was what I had always wanted, national exposure on a highly rated, popular news program. Life in the big city. A chance to live it up, travel, meet exciting people.

But none of it excited me or lit me up on the inside like I had always imagined it would. In fact, none of it interested me in the slightest. I would work, go home, binge Netflix until I fell asleep, and then wake up and do it all again the next day.

Then when I added thoughts of Hudson into the mix, things went from depressing to downright disastrous. I had completely and totally mishandled the entire situation with him. No one knew better than me just how hard it was to open up to someone the way we had with each other.

We told each other things we had never told another soul. We discovered things about ourselves that we had never known before. And we reached heights of sexual pleasure that I didn't know were even humanly possible.

And then I just got up and left.

It was so cold and clinical. Was that who I was, someone who could be that career-focused, that calculated? Was I really the type of guy that only thought about what I wanted, and not the needs of the person I cared most about?

I looked into the small mirror on the wall and tried smiling to cheer myself up. Then stopped almost straight away. I really hated my face. If there was ever a time in my life that I needed to be able to recognize my own goddamn face when I looked in the mirror, this was it. I couldn't even rely on that anymore.

"And then there's Mrs. Langley." Parker's words shook me from my own reflection.

I turned to look at him. Hearing him say her name brought my thoughts back to Daylesford, and my old life there, once again.

"What has Mrs. Langley got to say?" I asked, and for the first time in a long time, I was genuinely curious.

"It's all good, from what I can tell," Parker said, his eyes running across the page. "Oh."

He scrunched his nose up.

"What?" I asked nervously. "What is she saying?"

"Hmm," Parker said, taking off his glasses. "She's happy about pretty much everything, so that's good. But...she doesn't like the tooth thing, and she doesn't like..."

"Come on, Parker, stop dragging this out," I pleaded. The guy was killing me.

Parker cleared his throat and sat up a little straighter.

"She doesn't like that you and Hudson broke up. She said that she could tell that there was something special between you. Damnit," he said, dabbing at the corners of his eyes. "It's these new contacts."

He smiled awkwardly.

"Uh, Parker..." He looked up at me. "You're wearing your glasses today."

"Well, in that case," he said, shuffling over toward me. "Fuck you and fuck your love life for making me cry. I am not a pretty crier."

I was about to throw another smart-ass comment at him, when there was a knock on the door. We both looked at each other and shrugged. I certainly wasn't expecting anyone. Parker opened the door.

"Hi, is Liam here?" said a man's voice, and I saw Parker's confused expression spread out across his face.

"And you are...?"

"I'm a friend...of Hudson's."

Parker turned to me, wide-eyed and with his nose scrunched up even more than usual. I nodded and waved for him to let the guy in.

"I'll, uh, catch you later, Liam?" Parker said as he left, and a well-built, well-dressed man entered the room.

"I'm Porter," he said. He looked around the room, eyeing it in a way that showed he was clearly unimpressed.

"Hi, I'm..."

"I know who you are, Liam," he interrupted. "Believe you me, I really didn't want to drag my ass from Daylesford to New York City to see you."

"Oh, okay," I said as I pointed to a chair.

He shook his head. "I'll stand, thanks."

"So, why did you come here then?" I asked.

The man was all fire and attitude. Had Hudson sent him?

"I'll keep this brief," Porter said, reeking of *get me the fuck out of here* vibes. "I don't like you for a number of reasons. But...my friend does."

"Does he?"

Porter looked at me like I was the biggest idiot, but I wasn't being facetious. I was really asking. Did Hudson seriously still like me?

We had left so much unsaid. My last two weeks in Daylesford went by in such a blur that I could barely remember any of it now. It felt like a lifetime ago.

"Yes, he does," Porter said as he reached into the inside of his jacket. He pulled out a crumpled up piece of paper and handed it to me. "Here. See for yourself."

With one final disapproving look at me and around my broom closet of a dressing room, Porter huffed, turned on his heel, and left, closing the door loudly behind him.

With my mind still trying to process the whole weird interaction, I unfolded the piece of paper and looked at it.

It was a list entitled *18 things I like about Liam Wright*.

My heart rose to my throat, and then slammed back down again. I was instantly transported back to Hudson's gym and the conversation we had at our first workout session. The one where he'd joked—or at least I had thought it was a joke—that my ass was, like, his eighteenth favorite thing about me.

But the list I was holding in my hand was no joke.

I didn't know whether to smile or cry as I read the list, so I did both.

The loving tenderness of the man leaped from the page and made me want to be with him so much that it hurt to breathe.

I looked up at my reflection again in the mirror. The tiredness. My face caked with makeup. My unrecognizable smile.

I got hot and sweaty, but also felt a cold shiver run through me at the same time.

The walls of my miniscule dressing room were closing in on me with every haggard breath I was taking.

I had to get out. I had to leave. I had to go back and fix this.

I grabbed my backpack off the floor and slid my forearm across my dressing table, scooping everything I could into the bag. I zipped it up hastily as I walked out of the room.

I looked over my shoulder before I left, at the tiny, dimly lit dressing room. It didn't symbolize the fulfillment of my lifelong dream; it was the stuff of nightmares. A sign that I had pursued a dream so blindly and with such tunnel vision, that I couldn't even see that I didn't want it anymore.

Somewhere along the way, I had lost sight of who I was and what I *really* wanted to do with my life. I had become so disconnected from myself that I'd accepted the promotion without even properly considering it.

Because, if I had taken just one freaking moment to really think about it, I wouldn't have taken it. Not when I had discovered the one truly important thing that I wanted more than anything else.

Love.

And the man who had made me see that it was possible for me to be loved.

I stepped out onto the floor and tried to find Parker, but couldn't. Oh well, I would text him later and pray that he would understand. I got into the elevator and rode it all twenty-eight floors down to the ground.

Before I stepped out of the building and back into the hustle and bustle of New York, I looked down at the piece of paper I had clutched in my hand the entire time.

Hudson's list.

Was I doing the right thing?

I looked at the very last point. Number eighteen.

He's going to make a difference and leave the world a better place.

Damn right I was.

CHAPTER TWENTY-FOUR

HUDSON

"You want to know why I think your business is going down?" Porter asked through the wall of the shower cubicle.

I turned the water off, grabbed my towel and dried myself.

"Tell me, Porter, please. I'm dying to know," I said, barely able to contain my sarcasm.

"Open showers," Porter said as we each stepped out of our respective shower cubicles with our towels wrapped around our waists.

"Huh?"

We had just finished an impressive ninety-minute workout. Out of the quad squad, I had to admit Porter probably had the most well-proportioned and well-defined body. Not that I was checking him out, definitely not. Porter was like a brother to me—a younger, annoying one who I sometimes wanted to kick the living shit out of. There was no way on earth I'd ever look at him that way.

I was simply lamenting the waste of having such a good body

and literally zero ink over any of it. It was a damn shame. And believe me, I'd tried to convince him to get a tattoo, even a small one somewhere discreet and where no one else could see it. But Porter could be incredibly pigheaded and stubborn when he wanted to be, and for whatever reason, he was adamant that he wasn't interested in tattoos. At all.

"Open showers," Porter repeated. "Gyms that have open showers attract more clients. Or at least, more gay clients. Do you know how many times I've fucked dudes at the BodyWorks gym near my work?"

"No, and I don't want to know," I said as I saw Porter opening his mouth, about to regale me with yet another sexcapade.

"Porter, it's the twenty-first century," I continued. "With cell phones and social media, open showers just aren't practical anymore. There are too many creeps and weirdos who would do creepy and weird things if we had open showers."

"Well I think they're hot," Porter said, continuing to dry himself off and speaking as if we were actually having a serious discussion about the topic, which we were not. "And I'm not a creep or a weirdo, thank you very much."

Hmm, the jury was still out on that one.

"And besides," I said as I opened up my locker, grabbed my briefs, and slid them up my legs under my towel, much to Porter's amusement. "People come into the shower area to, you know, shower. Not to fuck."

Porter rolled his eyes as he took off his towel and stood naked in front of me, looking over at me with an unmistakable smirk stretching his lips. We had been through this routine a million times before, and I knew better than to give him what he was wanting from me—a reaction. Just because I turned red more often than a traffic light around the guy that I liked, didn't mean that Porter would have the same effect on me. I had a built up immunity to the guy and his constant sexual ribbing.

Not wanting to see my friend naked, or have him see me naked, didn't mean I was a prude. But after twenty years of knowing each other, the message still hadn't sunk in for Porter, who was quite happily swinging his dick in front of me, and the other four or five guys in the locker room. I ignored him and avoided looking at the man as best I could, like I had done a million times before and would probably do a million times again.

As annoying as he could be sometimes—and believe me, he could be plenty annoying—our twice-a-week workouts together were something that I very much looked forward to, Porter's seedy locker room chatter aside.

It had been almost a month since Liam had left, and after Porter's mini-intervention at my place two weeks ago, I knew I had to turn my life around.

That meant no more booze, no more morning TV programs, and definitely no booze while watching morning TV. I even got back to clean eating and getting serious about working out.

After all, I knew better than most that working out at the gym wasn't just good for physical fitness, it also improved mental health immensely. But I also knew just how easy it was to forget that and slip back into old, comfortable, unhealthy habits.

The loss of Liam still stung like a motherfucker. How could it not? Opening myself up to him like that had made it impossible to go back to the life I'd had before I met him.

I was pissed, but not at him, more at myself. That I had been such an idiot and not read the signs that were all around me. I mean, even Porter had warned me about the guy, and I chose to ignore his advice.

I had simply imagined it all.

That was probably the hardest part for me to reconcile. While I was sharing the most intimate and deepest parts of myself with Liam, he was simply going through the motions, happy to be adding to the believability of our fake relationship.

I stuffed my sweaty gym gear into my backpack and started to zip it up.

"How are you holding up?" Porter asked as he came over to me
—fully dressed, thankfully. "About Liam, I mean."

I let out a sigh.

"I'm...okay?" My voice was shaky. I looked up at Porter, and in
that moment, I needed his reassurance. I needed someone who
knew me as well as he did to confirm that I was, indeed, alright.
"Right?"

"Yeah, you're okay," Porter said with a friendly smile. "Or at
least, you will be one day."

I smiled and felt a little better.

"What about you, Mr. Jones?" I asked in a not-subtle-at-all
attempt to change the topic. "That guy out there in the free weights
area, Cameron, he was checking you out something fierce."

"Can you blame him?" Porter tilted his face to the side and gave
a cocky smile.

I shook my head. "You're unbelievable...but I can have a quiet
word with him if you like?"

"Hey, no more interfering." Porter wagged his finger at me.
"Wasn't that the rule?"

"Alright, alright, I won't say anything," I said with a grin. Then I
added under my breath, "Only trying to help."

"I appreciate the thought," Porter continued. "But you know
me. With my work, I have to be super careful. I can't afford a
scandal. It's either guys I meet at Revolver or one-time-only
hookups on apps. That's it."

"Is that what you want, though?" I asked, trying to hide the
frown I was sure I was sporting.

"It has to be," he shrugged, but I could hear the sliver of sadness
in the way he said it.

Porter might have been well versed at putting on a show of
bravado with all of his sexual adventures, but that's exactly what it
was—a show. Underneath all of that was a real person, and all
people need love. In whatever freaky or unconventional way feels
right for them.

"You wanna grab a bite?" Porter asked. Now it was his turn to change the topic of conversation.

"Sounds good," I said.

Well, it sounded better than eating at home alone.

We made our way out of the locker room and to the exit when my heart stopped beating.

Standing there, at the front desk, was Liam.

"Uh oh," Porter said.

I glared over at him, and saw his face was riddled with guilt and apprehension.

"I, uh, might have interfered," Porter whispered as we got closer to Liam.

In some ways, Liam looked exactly the same. It had only been a month, so it's not like we hadn't seen each other for years and could barely recognize each other. But there was something different about him. I couldn't quite put my finger on what it was though.

He saw us approaching and smiled.

His smile was different.

How, I couldn't quite tell yet, but thankfully, my heart had started beating again so I at least had enough strength to ask, "What are you doing here, Liam?"

Liam looked at me and blinked a few times, and then he turned to Porter and said, "You didn't tell him?"

Porter let out what sounded like a squeak and shook his head. "No, I didn't."

"Tell me what?" I growled. "Can someone please fill me in on what the hell is going on here?"

Porter shuffled his feet. "I flew to New York last weekend to speak with Liam and..."

"And what?" I demanded through clenched teeth.

"...and gave him something."

"This," Liam said as he stepped closer to me.

We were face to face for the first time in weeks, and my skin instantly felt like it was on fire standing so close to him. The good kind of fire, like the *sitting around a campfire with friends on a clear summer night and roasting marshmallows* kind of fire.

I looked down at the piece of paper he was holding.

"Is that my...?"

He nodded, saving me from having to finish that question.

I was overwhelmed with emotions. What those emotions were, exactly, I couldn't tell. It was a heady mixture for sure, relief mixed with confusion, mixed with anger. And so many unanswered questions.

As Liam Wright had a tendency to do whenever he walked into my gym, he had me both floored and speechless at the same time.

"Well, you sure took your sweet-ass time." The poisonous bitterness in Porter's words as he spat them out at Liam was unmissable.

"I literally left right after you did. I just packed up a few things and then came straight back."

"Nice try," Porter scoffed. "I was in New York a week ago, Liam. What, it's taken you a week to grow a conscience and a pair of balls?"

"Porter," I said in my low warning voice.

"What? It's true," Porter said, turning to me with pleading eyes.

I *hmpfed* on the inside. I was torn. I knew Porter had my best interest at heart, but on the other hand, Liam was standing less than a foot away from me.

"I left straight away," Liam said, the genuineness written all across his face. "I bought a van and drove to Daylesford that very day."

He bought a van?

He drove all the way from New York?

"Can—can we get out of here and talk, Hudson?" He flashed a smile, and that was when I saw it. That was what was different about him. He had fixed the crooked tooth, the one that, in my opinion, didn't need fixing. I loved his smile just as it always had been. It suited him and made him so perfectly unique.

"Are you okay if I take a rain check on that meal, Porter?"

"Don't think I have much choice, but...fine," he said. His words came out angrier than he meant them to.

I patted him on the shoulder. "Thanks."

I looked over at Liam, into his dark gray eyes, and felt as if I were about to jump off a cliff.

"Alright," I said with a haggard breath. "Let's go somewhere and talk."

Given the nature of the conversation we were going to have, I didn't feel comfortable going to a bar, or anywhere in public, really. So Liam and I ended up at my place.

"Did you want a drink or something?" I asked as we walked into my kitchen. I opened the fridge door. "I don't have any alcohol, but I've got some soda or juice if you like."

"No, I'm good, thanks," Liam said as he tentatively sat down at the table. I joined him a moment later.

"I'm sorry for everything that's happened. I want to come back and I want to be with you."

The words gushed out of Liam's mouth like a waterfall, before I even had a chance to say anything.

"I don't understand," I said, completely taken aback. "You left, Liam. You have a job and a new life in New York now. Why would you want to leave all of that, everything you've worked so hard for, just to come back here?"

Liam reached out and delicately folded his fingers around mine. His touch slowed my breath and soothed my beating heart.

"You," he said as a single tear fell from his eye.

I pulled my hand back sharply. "You can't give up everything you've worked your whole life for because of me, Liam. That won't work. Trust me."

"I'm not going to have to give anything up, Hudson," Liam said, attempting a confident smile as he brushed away his tear. "I'm a man with a van and a plan."

Our eyes met and we both burst out laughing at the same time. The sweetness of his laughter rang in my ears, and I instantly felt lighter and happier being with him.

"The rhyming was completely unintentional, I assure you," Liam said when we had finally settled. "But I am serious. I learned a lot in New York."

"Oh yeah, like what?" I was curious to hear this.

"Are you ready for a super cheesy cliché to come your way?" he asked with a grin.

"Coming from you?" I said with a smile. "I think I'm ready for anything."

At least, I fucking hoped so.

Liam looked around my kitchen and took a breath. "I realized that life is too short to not do what you really want to be doing with it."

He looked over at me and smiled, his now perfectly straight smile.

"You can relax, that was the cheesy part."

I pretended to wipe the sweat off my forehead. "Phew. That wasn't so bad."

"And I also realized," he continued, "clear as day, in fact, that I was doing so much of what I didn't want to be doing in my life, and missing out on the things that I really, truly did want."

His words stabbed at my chest. I was fighting against the temptation to think that any of this was about me...or us.

"So I quit my job and bought a van."

I wasn't sure which part of that statement was more shocking. "You quit?"

"Right after Porter left," he said with a firm nod as a steely look of determination filled his eyes.

"But, Liam, why? That job meant the world to you."

"It did...at one point." His whole body started to rock gently, as if he were willing the words to come to him. "But for a long time, it hasn't been about the work anymore. It's been all of these stupid things I was doing to get attention and get ahead. Stupid catchphrases, ridiculously tight pants, and even..."

"A fake relationship?" I offered glumly, falling back into my seat.

"Yes, even that." His words lingered in the air between us.

"But I don't think of it like that, what we had," he said. "It wasn't fake to me, Hudson. It was the realest thing I have ever experienced in my whole life."

I closed my eyes, slowly succumbing to all of the memories of Liam. No, I couldn't allow myself to do this. As much as I wanted to, as good as the pull toward him felt, I had to resist. It would only end in more pain and heartache. I was only just starting to get better.

"So you quit your job and bought a van," I said, opening my eyes. "And what's your plan?"

"Glad you asked." His eyes twinkled with glee. "As it turns out, all my crazy, stupid publicity efforts haven't gone unrewarded. I've got over one million followers on all of my social media channels combined, so screw New York and screw *Wake Up America*, because I don't need to be on TV."

"Right..." I still had no idea where he was going with any of this.

"So, I am going to do what I was meant to do with my life. Make a difference."

Our eyes met.

Of course, he'd read the list. I remembered writing that one, number eighteen. I knew from the moment I started crushing on him that there was more to him than he showed the world. And I knew he was meant to make a difference.

"I'm going to travel around the country and use my platform to highlight important issues. Whether it's drilling in Alaska, or rising sea levels in Florida, I am going to use the attention that I have garnered and do something good."

"Come for the ass, stay for the environmental issues," I said, and he threw his head back with laughter.

"I love it, yes! I might have to steal that and make it my new catchphrase."

"It's all yours," I said, more unsure than ever of what the hell was going on inside of me.

After a few moments of silence, I felt the energy between us shift again.

"Hudson?" Liam asked.

"Yes."

He chewed on his bottom lip. "Would you like to come with me?"

CHAPTER TWENTY-FIVE

LIAM

I thought waiting months for news about the promotion was torture, but the seconds of silence that fell between us after I asked Hudson if he would join me was a million times worse. His face gave away nothing, so I couldn't even imagine what he was thinking or feeling.

I knew it sounded completely crazy, throwing our lives away and packing everything into a van to travel around the country. But when the idea came to me, from literally out of nowhere, I knew that it was the right thing for me—and hopefully, for us.

"I–I think it sounds like a good plan," Hudson said when he finally, *finally* spoke. "I just don't understand why you want me to come with you."

"Because I love you, Hudson," I responded immediately.

Clearly I was having trouble keeping words in, but I was tired of keeping things in. Pushing my own feelings aside, repressing my desires...I was done with all of that.

I was determined to make the world a better place, and I wanted to do it with Hudson by my side.

"I have so much to tell you. We have so much to talk about, and so many details to figure out, I know that..."

I hesitated, suddenly hit by the realization that he could very well turn around and say no to all of this. I wouldn't have blamed him if he did, he had every right to be angry at me. I had left him and gone to New York, and I couldn't deny that even though I was doing what I had said I would do, a big part of it was a completely selfish move on my part.

But thankfully, Hudson gave me the best answer in the world.

He got up, walked over to me, and wrapped me up in his massive arms. I stood up as well and melted into his body, instantly regretting how long it had been since I had felt him like this.

He lifted my chin, our eyes locked, and then we kissed. It was sweet as much as it was sorrowful. His tongue licked against my lip, and I let out a small gasp as it dawned on me what was happening.

Hudson had always said that sex was more than just a physical thing for him, that it was a form of communication. That was what he was doing now, telling me through his body, not through his words.

He cupped his hands around my jaw to keep me still. I felt a woozy rush as I relinquished control to him. He needed this, to communicate to me exactly what he was thinking and feeling.

And I needed it to. Because it mattered to me, what was going on for him. A lot.

That had been my biggest mistake. Well, one of them at least. I was so caught up in all of my own stuff that it had prevented me from seeing what was right in front of me.

The best thing in the world.

A person who would love and accept me unconditionally.

A man who could, with his hands and mouth, take me to the outer limits of the universe. Or with his warm smile and friendly eyes, give me silent permission to moan, groan, splutter, yell, cry out, and release all of my unfiltered self in front of him.

And now here he was, holding me still and silent. He was reconnecting with me.

He brushed his tongue delicately across my upper lip. I could feel his sweet breath on me, but it wasn't as close as I wanted it to be, as I needed it to be.

I pulled back and looked deep into his light green eyes. I saw the reservation in his face. He was scared. I had hurt him.

I ran my hands across his chest, starting in the middle and making my way to his massive round shoulders. I pulled myself in closer and bit down on his neck. His head fell back, but he didn't moan. His silence was telling me he was still holding back.

I bit into his Adam's apple. Hard. I needed him to feel me and to know that this was real. I was back, and I wanted him back.

He ran his fingers through my hair, scraping my scalp before he tugged and pulled my head back. I smiled, but he frowned.

Oh right, my tooth. Damn, I knew it was a mistake to get it fixed. Hudson had always said how much he liked it, how much it suited me. I'd never had a problem with it either, but ironically, now that it was perfect, I did.

My smile turned apologetic as I smashed my mouth into his. I wanted him to feel me, to taste me, to know that I wanted him. My tongue dove into his mouth and swirled around like a tornado, exploring every part of him. I pinched the fingers of one hand into his neck, and with the other, I grabbed at his Adam's apple, applying just enough pressure to make my presence felt.

He wasn't responding to any of it. He wasn't pulling away, either, but he just stood there, like a lump. The paralyzing fear of having lost him, that it was already too late, ran up my spine, and I stopped.

I let go of his neck, his Adam's apple, and slowly retreated from his mouth. My withdrawal was an acknowledgement of defeat.

Just as I was about to pull away, I felt his strong hand at the arch of my lower back. My skin prickled with heat, and I hoped against all hope that he wasn't going to let me go. He didn't.

Hudson pulled me back into his arms, pressed the side of my face against his heated chest, his fingers running through my hair and down my back, over and over and over again. He was soothing me.

He had let me do what I needed to do, show him the urgency of what I was experiencing and that my feelings for him were real and stronger than ever before.

And he had done what he had needed to do. He gave me that space, but he also made me realize that I had caused him pain. I knew I couldn't just come back here and pick things up where we had left them. That wasn't what I wanted, anyway.

I wanted more.

His momentary unresponsiveness was his way of showing me that. Besides, the man was probably still processing, and in a bit of shock too. Again, these were all things that I needed to know and that he was telling me, without saying a word, without even moving a muscle.

But now I was in his arms and he was telling me, with every breath he took, that I could feel in his rising and falling chest, and with every stroke of his steady hand through my hair and down my back, that we were going to be okay. That there was a chance that we would make it after all.

I let myself sink further into the moment. The joy of being with him, the sacredness of what we had between us, the sheer joy of simply being young, healthy, and alive. It coursed through my veins and made me feel all sorts of wonderful. I closed my eyes and silently prayed this moment could last forever.

Eventually, I gently peeled myself away and looked up into those shining light green eyes of his.

"So, will you do it?" I asked breathlessly. "Will you come with me and travel the country in the van?"

"I will," Hudson replied calmly, but there was nothing calm

about the fireworks it set off in my chest. "But first, I want to hear you say it."

"Say what?"

"That this...is real."

"Oh, my beautiful Hudson," I said, cupping his face in my hands. "This is the realest thing that's ever existed."

His eyes exploded with love and an overwhelming joy that I could feel radiating off his body.

"And you know," I said as I traced my fingers over his bicep and to the yellow ink on his arm, covering his first ever tattoo. "I'm always right."

EPILOGUE

HUDSON

"What about that one over there?" Liam raised his hand, pointing to the far right.

"Hmm..." I replied thoughtfully. It really did just look like a blob of white and fluffy gray, but I couldn't exactly say that. I finally settled on, "Pensiveness."

"Huh?"

Liam turned his head as a strand of hair fell across his forehead, stopping just above his beautiful gray eyes. I reached over and playfully brushed the wayward hair aside.

"Yeah, like the feeling of when you want to say something but you can't. So you hold yourself back, but you still can't shake that energy of wanting to say it."

Liam slowly turned his head back to the sky, and inspected the cloud in question one more time, before turning his gaze back on me. "Yeah, okay. I can see that."

He broke out into a wide smile as he grabbed my hand and

pressed my fingers to his lips, running his tongue seductively over my fingertips. He gently lapped at them, getting them just the right amount of slick, before pulling my hand down toward his nipple.

He loved it when I played with his nipples.

I ran my wet fingers around in small circular motions, before giving him a gentle squeeze with my thumb and index finger. His whole body shuddered against the ground we were lying on.

I loved seeing him so free and open. I let go of his nipple and brought my hand back to my side. The look of loss on his face was immediate.

I cleared my throat.

"Your turn," I said, turning my attention to the deep blue Colorado sky we were lying under. We were a few hours' drive out from Denver and had decided to pull over for some lunch and a little bit of midday sky-gazing. Because we could.

It was seventy degrees, but a breezeless and warm seventy, so we'd decided to take our shirts off and lie down on them. Because we could.

I looked over at Liam, who was busily staring up at the sky, smattered with an array of all sorts of clouds. I ran my still moist finger over his protruding hip bone, knowing just how much he loved it. Because I could.

"That one, there," he said, pointing directly above us.

"The one that looks like a penis?" I asked, chuckling.

"I would have gone for a milk bottle, but whatever," he laughed back. "No, the one to the right of that one."

"Ah, yeah," I said as my eyes focused in on the medium-sized, puffy white cloud.

"That one feels like...hope. I mean, I know it's technical name is a cumulus, but that one feels hopeful somehow."

"How?" I pressed.

I loved giving him little challenges and seeing how he would respond.

For someone who had always been so in control, who so

carefully curated what he showed the world, seeing Liam unfiltered and out of his comfort zone was the most thrilling thing in the world for me.

And believe me, spending the last six months traveling across the country cramped together in a van had thrown up plenty of opportunities for us both to step out of our comfort zones. Not that I would have changed a minute of it for the world.

Agreeing to join Liam on this adventure was the best decision I had ever made.

"It's just so light," he began, drawing my attention to the cloud he was talking about. "There's nothing but white and...goodness. No dark spots, nothing menacing. And that's how I feel when I'm hopeful. That there's only good ahead, and no bad."

I turned onto my side and rested on my elbow, running my finger through the smattering of light hairs on his lower abdomen. His eyes rolled into the back of his head, and a soft sound escaped from his lips.

"You know exactly what I'm talking about, don't you?" he finally asked.

I did.

I slowly teased him, dragging my fingers across the flesh of his belly, back up to the nipple I had just played with. I flicked it playfully, and his face softened into a look of heavenly bliss.

Over the past six months, we had developed our own language. One meant *yes*. One pinch, one kiss, one touch, one squeeze.

Two meant *no*.

Three meant *give it to me harder and don't stop until I tell you to*.

Three was definitely my favorite.

I lay back down and stared up at the sky again, letting the contentment and peace I was feeling wash all over me.

My life had changed since Liam came back, and all of it was good...and hopeful.

I ended up selling the gym to Zander. It was time to let that part of my life go. His heart was in it, mine wasn't. I knew he would build on the momentum we had gotten from Liam promoting the gym, and if anyone could restore it back to its former glory, I knew it would be him.

I managed to invest all of the money from the sale, and given our low-frills lifestyle, was able to live off the interest it earned.

I also started studying psychology. It was an online course, so as long as I had Wi-Fi, I was good to go. Caffeine helped as well, of course.

But most important of all, I had Liam by my side. I had meant what I'd said when he came back to Daylesford. I didn't want him giving his dream up for me. Sure, it would have been a grand romantic gesture, but over time, he would have grown to resent me. That was the last thing I wanted.

But this way, his crazy plan to buy a van and travel throughout the country meant that neither one of us was giving anything up. I was pursuing the change I had wanted to make for a while by studying psychology, and he was able to use his massive platform to highlight the issues that really mattered to him.

We had already visited a marine rehabilitation centre in Southern California, joined a series of environmental rallies in Seattle, and we were just coming out of a week-long climate change conference in Denver. Along the way, we got to experience just how big and beautiful this country really was.

And we got to make love, our way—our unique, special, sacred way—all over this spectacular country of ours.

"You know," Liam said, almost absent-mindedly, as he continued staring at the sky above us. "This really is all because of you, Hudson."

I opened and closed my mouth a few times, unsure of what to say. His words jarred me, but in the best possible way. I turned away and took a few deep breaths myself. Tears of happiness were welling up behind my eyes at those words. Those seemingly casual words of his that had hit me smack bang in the middle of my chest.

They mixed with the words that Richie had written to me.

This isn't because of you.

They were like water and oil in my soul.

Richie had been right, and I knew what he'd intended by writing that. He was trying to alleviate the pain he knew his actions would cause me.

And hearing Liam say what he'd said felt right too. It felt more than right, actually. It felt like he was revealing an ultimate truth.

I wasn't going to be alone.

My unconventional sexual interests didn't mean I was destined to not find another person I could share them with. Because with Liam, I'd found someone who was on the exact same wavelength.

I still wasn't able to put my thoughts into words, and as I looked across at him, I could see his eyes becoming unfocused and his breathing slowing down. At this rate, he'd be asleep and lightly snoring in no time.

I took his long, slender fingers in my hand. I needed to tell him what I was feeling, just how much the words he had uttered had affected me so deeply.

But I didn't want to just tell him.

I squeezed down on his hand.

One.

Two.

Three.

~

LIAM

A fierce heat tore through me as I felt Hudson squeeze my hand three times. I knew exactly what that meant. My cock did too, stiffening instantly at the inevitability of where this was heading.

I slowly opened my eyes and looked down to make sure I wasn't dreaming. Nope, Hudson's fingers were definitely wrapped around mine. That squeeze I had felt was as real as the ground we were lying on.

I turned my gaze to the man and stared into Hudson's eyes. The usual lightness wasn't there. Instead, I was met with an intensity that I wasn't expecting.

I was just about to ask if something was wrong, when he let go of my hand and gently brushed his fingers along my cheek reassuringly. I opened my mouth and let my breath escape me.

He was communicating. He had something to share, something he wanted me to know.

I kept focusing on my breathing, as he had told me to do so many times over the last six months. I steadied myself with every deep breath in, and with every long exhale out. I tried to put all the other thoughts in my mind to rest.

But it wasn't easy.

Not that my thoughts were bad or filled with anxiety as they used to be. No, now my thoughts were more like clouds, floating in and out of my mind gently and peacefully. It was comforting and joyful at the same time. That gnawing feeling deep inside me that I was on the wrong track, doing the wrong things, was totally gone. It had been replaced by...hope.

And the love of a truly wonderful, patient, inspiring man.

Even though van life was my idea, I had been slightly petrified as we drove out of Daylesford that sunny Sunday morning. I had, after all, done a complete life turnaround. I'd thrown away the only thing I had ever wanted and worked so hard for. My career.

I could still remember Parker's voice over the phone as he was pleading, yelling, saying anything he possibly could to get me to change my mind. But I was done with that part of my life. The crazy publicity-seeking stunts, the scheming, the plotting, always to get attention, but never for anything real.

Parker stayed in New York and, thankfully, managed to land on his feet. He picked up a few new clients from the network, and things with his new guy—who happened to be called Jack—were progressing nicely. From what I gathered from his last email, things with both of his Jacks were going nicely.

As excited as I was to embark on this new adventure, and despite it feeling right on a deep soul level, I was petrified that it would all blow up in my face. And sure, I did lose some followers, but then again, I picked up a ton more.

Despite some initial hesitation from people in positions of power in the environmental movement, I was slowly but surely picking up more sponsorships and paid gigs. Luckily our main expenses were fuel and food, and I could still easily cover that.

I felt Hudson's fingers impatiently tugging at the waistband of my shorts. He got himself up, resting on his knees and haunches as he unbuttoned my shorts and opened my fly slowly.

I had started freeballing—actually, we both had,—since we'd started travelling together. It meant one less thing to wash, and one less layer between us.

He slid my shorts halfway down my thighs and my hard cock flung out and slapped itself against my stomach with a hearty *thwack*. Hudson smiled deliciously as he ran his thumb over the precum that had landed on my belly, using the wetness to rub along the tip of my nipple.

God, he knew me and my body, so well.

"Any requests?" he said with a smile as his fingers eased into a gentle, familiar, but still super fucking hot crowning. My whole body vibrated with pleasure from his touch.

"Corkscrew," I said without hesitation. He let out a hearty laugh.

"That's become your favorite, hasn't it?"

I nodded. "Can you blame me? The way you do it is so fucking good, Hudson."

A slight blush rose to his cheeks, but it suited him. He wasn't embarrassed, I could tell. He was proud.

He began a very delicate version of the corkscrew, twisting his wrist over the head of my cock as he slid his hand down and back up along my entire length, only to twist his wrist the other way. It was one of the most pleasurable sensations ever. The inconsistency and varying pressures of the movement always drove me wild, and guaranteed a strong orgasm.

After a few strokes, he stopped and looked me straight in the eye.

"What you said before," he began. "About how this is all because of me. Well, that meant a lot to me, Liam."

I cupped my hands around his face and he twisted to kiss them.

"It's true," I said as I beamed at him.

"You saw things in me before you even knew me. And you believed in me at a time when I had stopped believing in myself. If Porter hadn't shown me that list..."

My head flung back as Hudson's mouth landed on my cock and he sucked me down. There was an intensity to his movement as his shaved head bobbed up and down on my cock.

I interlaced my fingers against the back of his smooth head. He knew what I wanted. He slowed down, still taking me down to my base, but he was getting himself ready at the same time.

After a few more long strokes, I felt his fingers tracing up my side, almost tickling me, as they landed on my left nipple. He gave me three firm pinches.

I smiled as I forced my cock all the way down his throat, my fingers pressing his head against my body. I could feel his acceleration along my lower abdomen. Hudson made the sweet gurgling sound that he knew drove me wild, as he hummed against the tip of my cock.

I had discovered that I enjoyed getting deepthroated...a lot. And since I had been learning to overcome shame, I shared what I had discovered with Hudson, who, to my great delight, was very eager to give me exactly what I wanted.

Which, right now, was this man's mouth filled with my cock,

and his nose pressed against my stomach. I wrapped my legs around his waist and pushed him down farther on my cock.

This closeness, this connection, this was pure unadulterated freedom. I never thought I would get a chance to experience it. But here I was, living my best life, driving across the country with the man who's every breath, every flick of the tongue, I could feel on my cock.

A man who had unleashed parts of me that I'd thought were destined to stay buried forever.

A person who saw through all of my surface-level bullshit to the real me I was hiding underneath.

And when he saw it, when he saw all of me and who I was—the good, the bad, the weird, and the ugly—he didn't flinch. Not even for a moment.

He just loved me. All of me.

And I loved him too.

More than anything in the world. He was my rock, my best friend, my teacher and guide, and the man who showed me that anything was possible in life—including being able to come eight times in a row.

At least for now. I was hoping to get into double digits by Christmas.

Our original plan for the day was to make it to a small eco resort about forty miles away. But with what we had just started, I had a feeling we wouldn't get there until well after sundown.

And I was perfectly fine with that.

THE END

ABOUT CASEY COX

Contemporary/New Adult MM Romance Author

Casey Cox is devoted to delighting readers with sassy, sweet and sometimes steamy MM gay romance tales of gorgeous, good-hearted and complex men chasing that thing we all love: a guaranteed HEA.

Casey lives on the east coast of Australia, loves the beach and is a proud fur-parent to two utterly adorable, perfectly-perfect French Bulldogs named Ralphie and Lilly.

For more information, please visit
www.caseycoxbooks.com